I0639181

MURDER STORY

MURDER STORY

Agata Stanford

A JENEVACRIS PRESS PUBLICATION

MURDER STORY
JUNE 2014

PUBLISHED BY
JENEVACRIS PRESS
NEW YORK

This is a work of fiction. Names, characters, places, and
incidents either are the product of the author's imagination
or are used fictitiously. Any resemblence to actual persons,
living or dead, events, or locales is entirely coincidental.

———◆———

All rights reserved
Copyright © 2014 byAgata Stanford
Edited by Shelley Flannery
Typesetting and Cover Design by Eric Conover

ISBN 978-0-9857803-3-3

Printed in the United States of America

www.dorothyparkermysteries.com

*For my good friends, Eric Conover
and Shelley Flannery*

Also by Agata Stanford

The Dorothy Parker Mystery Series:
The Broadway Murders
Chasing the Devil
Mystic Mah Jong
Death Rides the Midnight Owl
A Moveable Feast of Murder
The Murder Club

MURDER STORY

The greatest evil is conceived and ordered in clean, carpeted, warmed, and well-lighted offices, by quiet men with white collars and cut fingernails and smooth-shaven cheeks who do not need to raise their voice.

—C. S. Lewis

"...and if you wrong us, shall we not revenge?"

—Shylock, Act III, Scene I,
The Merchant of Venice

Chapter One

When I was five, I watched my father kill my mother.

Alone—my father quit the city to places unknown never to be seen again—I was sent to live with my mother's elderly aunt and her husband for a short time. At her death, less than a year later, my uncle, unable to cope with the needs of a child, shuffled me off to the Orphans Asylum on Fifth Avenue. I had not spoken a word since witnessing my mother's violent end, so it was believed that I was "slow." It came as a great surprise to everyone when I suddenly spoke up to correct a teacher's misstatement. I might have been thrashed had I not referred to the text, paragraph, and line number, to support my case, and except for the amazement of the teacher at the sound of my voice. Soon, it was discovered that I was quite clever, with an artistic bent. Mine was not a Dickensian existence; I did not suffer the cruelty imposed upon Oliver Twist. But for the taunting of a few vicious boys, my jailors were kindly, if strict, the life regimental, and I accepted their indifference as well as my circumstances as a cross to bear in this life. I was born to Jewish parents, but that did not stop the nuns from drilling into me the love of Our Savior, Jesus Christ. Yearning for acceptance, I dutifully learned my prayers well and gave thanks for the meager sustenance provided for me. When I was older, I was taught a trade, and because I had no love for draftsmanship, I found employment and excitement instead at the *Herald* as a messenger boy. I was fifteen and on my own and determined to become a great newspaperman. My love of the tabloids was unrequited, however. Murder, not of the barroom-brawl variety but the more lascivious sort—sex, greed, jealousy, and murder at a good address—was the order of the day and commanded the headlines.

As a copyboy, I had dreams of becoming a reporter. I thrilled as I observed the camaraderie among the brash, clever, fast-talking men who covered the news—and those new foreign correspondents reporting from the war in France or from the Revolution in Russia in '17, coming home with their stories, padded with fabricated acts of heroism, no doubt, but swallowed whole all the same by the likes of me. They'd frequent the saloon down the block from the paper, and they'd let me join them for a beer. How I wanted to be like them! How I worshipped these big, rough and rumple-suited, hard-drinking men! For a time I basked in the warmth of familial belonging; they'd ruffle my hair or squeeze my shoulder affectionately and tell

me the ways of life and how to hone the craft of
reporting. I wanted to become one of them.

And I had my chance when the likely choice
to rush off and get the scoop on a murder was off
witnessing an execution at Sing-Sing, while other
reporters had been sent to cover an anarchist
bombing of a factory in New Jersey, a fire in Harlem,
and a freight train derailment on the Hudson. There
was only me, so the city editor reluctantly sent me
to cover the stabbing death of a shop-girl at the
mansion of a wealthy merchant on Fifth Avenue.

This was my chance! I practically flew uptown,
ready to make my name in print, imagining my
byline, the slaps on the back I'd receive from the
seasoned columnists as they bought me round after
round of boilermakers!

I saw the ravaged body of the young woman
and I threw up and fainted at the scene. No one from
my paper saw me. I was able to get the story, but
it was no different the third and fourth times I was
sent out to a murder scene. I'd become violently ill.
What could I say other than that it was a reaction to
the sight of blood, not an uncommon affliction? But
it wasn't just the sight of blood; it was the memory of
violent murder come back to torture me, and I could
not tell anyone the reason, about the evil my father
had set upon my mother. I felt shamed, nonetheless;
I wound up assigned as the assistant to the drama
critic, who bullied me into shape as a second-string
reviewer. Manhattan was a carnival of ongoing

entertainment, and I saw the great offerings of the Tenderloin during that first year with Alexander Woollcott, and for a while I indulged in carefree escape into a world I had never dreamed I might be a part of. But the War changed everything. Because I was classified unfit to serve, I remained at home. I became dissatisfied with the vacuous task of my job at a time of turmoil in Europe. When Woollcott went off to France to write for *Stars and Stripes*, I was not chosen to replace him in his absence, but remained second-string, assigned to review the Second Avenue Yiddish shows and the Vaudeville lineups. As second-string drama critic I became known around the newsroom as *Ersatz* Stringer, my surname lending itself to ridicule. I was young. I felt humiliated. Only the old press boys address me as Ersatz now, when our paths cross. Its implication always rankled in me, and even when spoken with affection I hear mockery.

So I realized I'd probably never be a great newspaperman. But I liked to write. I began to write my own stories. And then a book. Everything changed because of the book. I was not just relaying my observations of the adventures of the people of New York for a daily publication; *I* was creating the adventures for the first time.

Writing a book is like watching a silent movie. You think you know, but you don't know where it's all going to lead. The story unfolds in its own time, at its own pace, from beginning to end, like a life. Like a twisty-turning, uncharted life.

I see now that my life, too, is a book. A book I cannot edit. I can only hope to write a pleasant ending. Since we all die, there are no really happy endings.

The first sharp twist in the plot of my life was that night when I was five, the next, an imperceptible veering when I was thirty. That veering started in 1927 when I walked into Romany Marie's Café on Christopher Street. I wondered recently, what if I'd never entered Marie's? What if I had walked on to the Brevoort Café? Or Polly's Restaurant?

———◆———

Six authors we were, and of the others I had only slightly known Mark Wendt of the cowboy books, whom I had met briefly at a book party, and Daniel Cousins, who signed on with Niles Pickering around the time I did. Daniel's contract with Pickering had not been renewed, because he, like me, had failed to produce a publishable work of fiction for several years.

It was not long after the publisher's sudden death and the collapse of Pickering Press that I would occasionally stop in at Romany Marie's Café for a bowl of soup, which Marie Marchand, the middle-aged proprietress, garbed in gypsy fare, would generously provide as sustenance for some of us struggling artists. Marie has quite a distinctive face: dark, broad-jawed, determined, but not an unkind face. I could see her sizing up the physique of any newcomer to her establishment. Eyes scrutinizing from across the room, she seemed to measure the protrusion of a new arrival's shoulder blades through a threadbare coat, the absence of hose, the state of shoe-leather. Dimples creasing her wide mouth and a sparkle brightening her black eyes, she'd welcome her new patron, sit him down at a table, and bring him a steaming bowl of her husband's famous stew from the pot that was always simmering atop the woodstove. That man might be the starving alcoholic, Eugene O'Neill, when he was first trying to write a play, back during the winters of '16 and '17, before his great success on Broadway, or an enthusiastic, if malnourished, Buckminster Fuller, images of new designs for living playing out in his young head. Whoever frequented the café, young or old, rich or poor, there was always a warm welcome from Marie. In the winter, Marie's was a haven from my drafty flat a couple of blocks away, the woodstove radiating its smoky heat, the nutty aroma of café noir à la Turque permeating the toasty room.

In the evenings, when Cherish was working, I would pass the time there in the company of other artists, or those aspiring to be, often students or professors from New York University at Washington Square. Conversing with likeminded folk was stimulating entertainment—after a day spent alone with my typewriter—talking politics and philosophy. Sometimes, when I found myself without companionship, I might be entertained by eavesdropping on the most preposterous blather proffered by some horny old-coot instructor, playing the intellectual—beard, pipe, scarf rakishly tossed across his neck—hell-bent on impressing, and ultimately bedding, the nubile student he's managed to entrap at his table. The brighter of her sex would reject these lectures, designed to seduce by displaying the fellow's intellectual prowess, which was more often than not just a tired old thesis repeated semester after semester by rote, and remove the hand that had found its way to her knee and walk out of the café unscathed and uncompromised; the more gullible young doe might actually believe the blowhard's salacious leer to be a passion for the subject of his discourse, taking the tired "insights" as serious reflections of a superior mind. These scenes would be played out in the foreground of droned recitations of bad poetry and uninspired musical renditions limited to three chord sequences on the guitar.

"There's nothing more seductive than a brainy man," said Cherish once, many years ago, after my novel was published to good notices. She was talking about me, of course. And there is nothing more seductive for a man than when the woman you lust for *thinks* you a genius.

John French Sloan retires to the café at day's end; he keeps to a small circle of friends, and the portrait he painted of Marie a few years ago is hung over his favorite table. We usually nod politely at one another, but that's the extent of our acquaintanceship. And the beauty, poetess Edna St. Vincent Millay, frequents Romany Marie's. She wrote her little verse there, the one that begins: "My candle burns at both ends. . . ." There is an unfriendly aloofness about Vincent, who is very much aware of her ethereal appeal and expects it to be appreciated.

Late one afternoon in the spring of 1927, I was at Marie's when Daniel Cousins walked into the café. The fact that we were both castoffs from the Pickering "empire" was the only thing we had in common at the time. I suppose you might say misery loves company, so when I saw him walk in I invited him to join me.

Cousins has a head of unruly, black hair crowning heavy, slightly hangdog features. Still, there is a handsome ruggedness about him. Underlying this solid countenance is an air of melancholy to be seen in big, sad brown eyes, which lends a gentleness to his demeanor. Although a pleasant fellow, his initial reticence can be a bit off-putting. I came to understand that his seeming aloofness is not because he is unapproachable, but because he is innately shy. Eventually, he began to appear at Marie's more regularly, several times a week after work at his copy-editing job at the *Saturday Evening Post*, and soon I became privy to his personal history.

He was born in nineteen-hundred, in Providence, Rhode Island, the second son of two born to Italian-immigrant parents, Enrico and Carmella Cugini.

Daniel's father was a fishmonger who died of sepsis after he pricked a finger on a fishbone; his mother, a seamstress, now widowed, had found herself sole support of the family. Her sewing skills proved clever, and she was industrious. She pawned her late mother's jewelry, given to her by her father when she left the old country. She bought a few yards of fine silk and rented a room above a haberdasher's shop. With the bolts of satin ribbon and the lace she'd brought in her trousseau to America, she began designing and selling lingerie to the Newport crowd, which led to her remarriage to a wealthy widower. Because she was "in trade" as the proprietress of Carmella Lingerie she'd never been accepted by her husband's society friends, and within a year they were divorced. She was financially secure through her industrious business dealings, the divorce settlement was generous, and Carmella never had to sew a stitch again. But, as it was not in her nature to retire to a life of leisure, she expanded her business by opening stores in major cities across the country.

When I asked Daniel why he kept his copywriter's position at the *Saturday Evening Post*, he replied that he was too old to be supported by his mother and that the job offered him discipline, and was encouraged by Dr. Curry, the alienist he had been seeing twice a week for over a year, as beneficial to an artistic nature. He needed a place to go to each day, to do a simple job, to be responsible to others while he contemplated his next book. But, he—like myself—had been contemplating new ideas for books for a long time without much success. His one and only novel, one I consider a quiet little unobtrusive work of brilliance, was years in the past.

I told him how much I liked his debut novel and asked what he was currently at work on, but he mumbled something about how he'd been plagiarized, how he'd never trust leaving a manuscript with a publisher again.

Confused, I asked how and when and by whom his work had been stolen. He replied that an unscrupulous publisher to whom he had sent the novel, after having rejecting it, had published the book under the authorship of another writer a year later!

I was taken aback by this accusation, and when I said that it was outrageous, that there were laws, that he should sue, Daniel said that these nefarious people didn't use an identical sentence from his book when they lifted the theme, the plot, the characters, the general tone from his manuscript, so there was nothing, really, that he could do on the legal front. He'd paid for the best lawyers to look into it to no avail, so they got away with their thievery. Appalled, and a little disbelieving of his claim, I asked who had done such a thing?

"Jim Morrow published it; Frederick Feldman, a . . . *friend* of his, who never wrote anything other than a gardening column for the *Daily News*, passed my book off as his own."

The weighty implication of the word *friend* had me thinking. . . .

The other writer who frequented Romany Marie's, and who was also a Niles Pickering author, was Mark Wendt.

Mark is a good-looking fellow: mid-thirties, tall, blond, blue-eyed, with the grace of a dancer. There is an air of the theatrical about Mark, in the sense that when he enters a room, he commands attention with no visible effort at all. He appears to accomplish, with no conscious affectation, a seasoned actor's stage entrance.

I doubt it was conscious and calculated, but he would enter the café and stand in the doorway, eyes scanning the room, walking a silver dollar in and out through his fingers, and because of his natural charisma all eyes would turn toward him. He always gave the impression that he was glad to see me, that he had actually come to Marie's looking for me. I soon realized that that was not always the case. It was just his amiable, all-inclusive manner that he displayed with everyone he had known a passing acquaintance with. Women, especially women, the young and middle-aged ones, believed he held a special interest in them. I would watch their longing, lonely eyes turn at his entrance, and he would always smile and say their names when he moved past their tables nodding hello, perhaps offering a compliment for a jaunty hat, a well-adorned shawl, before moving on, table by table, working the room like a suave maître d' at the Waldorf.

Mark had had a career as a Broadway hoofer before taking up the pen, I found out as he slowly revealed bits and pieces of his life. Now, he was enjoying a string of successes writing Western novels, popular among adolescent boys and adventure-starved men, but I had heard through a friend that he wanted to be taken seriously as an author.

The first time we met at Romany Marie's was during the fall of '27, when I looked up from my notebook to see him approaching my table. He smiled boyishly, and asked if I remembered him, which of course I did, so I pulled out a chair. He was rolling a coin through his fingers, like a magician, and I asked him to show me how he did it. I fumbled and kept dropping the silver dollar on the table. Then, when I reached for it where I thought it had fallen, the coin was gone. Mark told me to check inside my shirt pocket, and there it was!

"Sleight of hand," he told me, "a magician's trick."

I said he was very talented, and he said that the coin trick had nothing to do with talent, just nimble fingers and lots of practice. "Writing, the way you do it, takes talent and a nimble mind, Ernest."

I was flattered when he looked at me with such an expression of reverence, and offered the most effusive praise of my work, of the book I'd written years ago to good reviews, but which had never had a second printing. This whispered veneration was unexpected and I felt a little thrill and a sudden lift of encouragement. I was a bit embarrassed, too, I admit, especially when he asked about my "process."

I thought to myself, *What process? I haven't got a process.* But, I kept mute.

I had come to believe that the book I had written, which was received with much praise from the critics, had been a fluke. Upon rereading it not long ago, I wondered who could have written something so true, so viscerally wrenching, so . . . profoundly *good*? I was coming to terms with the possibility that I was a one-shot wonder. Could I have once been that man, that acclaimed author, Ernest Stringer? Ernest Stringer . . .

What happened to Ernest Stringer, the author of *A Treasure of Tomorrows*? Were mine the very same fingers of its author, fingers that had tripped violently across the keys, tapping at sixty words a minute, words, dialogue coming through faster than I was capable of typing them out onto the page, fingers that these days fell ineffectively on the Royal's keyboard? What happened to the man whom one lofty reviewer acclaimed as "the modern Henry James"?

That was five years ago, and today I was a publishing business pariah, a flash-in-the-pan, not having produced anything worthwhile since.

I was tired of telling those well-meaning people who liked the book and would ask when the next was due to be published that I was busy at work on a new story, which was a lie, of course, an effort to buy time. "A writer doesn't like to talk about his work," would be my reply when asked its theme, knowing, dreading the truth: There was nothing at all I could find to say for another book.

With the events of those past few months leading up to the death of Niles Pickering, I had considered leaving Manhattan, settling in some small town where nobody knew me and trying my hand at selling insurance, rather than enduring the increasingly skeptical expressions on people's faces. I sensed that I was unconsciously projecting the desperation of a dried-up has-been as smiles stiffened and pitying silences replaced their prior admiration and enthusiasm. After a while, nobody asked what I was working on. That was worse. It was more demoralizing than I could stand much longer.

So, now, to steer the conversation away from the exalted alter-ego I had once been, and for lack of imagination, I brought up the untimely death of Niles Pickering.

Mark said that he had gone to the funeral, even though Pickering had not renewed his contract.

I admitted I had been dealt the same hand, but I said I was surprised that, before his death, Pickering would let go of such a prolific—as well as profitable—author such as he.

"Creative differences; I refused to write any more Cowboy books," he admitted, playing with the silver dollar. "Anyway, he had a plan in the works to turn his literary house into a pulp factory."

"What! Like cheap romance and gangster stories?"

"Right, like the stuff you see at the newsstands, magazines and cheap books."

Ah, I thought. It was Mark who had bolted from Pickering!

I was reticent about my situation. I, like Cousins, kept things close to the vest. But after a while, and because of Mark's candor, his desire to write important books, I confessed to Wendt that I was at a standstill in my career. When he asked how I managed without a steady income, I didn't tell him about the other stuff I had been hacking out for publisher Harvey Price, whose hidden subsidiary published decidedly salacious fare, worse than the pulp magazines at the newsstands. No, the books I was hacking out could never be displayed to the general public. They were for a distinctly different audience. These sex stories kept food in my mouth and a roof over my head, though I was loath to admit I was the man behind the moniker, Lance Pierce! I had Price's assurance that no one would *ever* know it was I who was writing this trash. Only Cherish knew.

Mark said that he wished he could write as well as I.

Here was a man entertaining thousands of readers with well-written novels about the Old West, while I was just a one-shot deal. Mark Wendt said he "wanted to be more; he wanted to be an *artist* like me. I found his admission disconcerting. He'd found a niche and was a success; I was struggling, writing trash, and had no real vision for my future. Ashamed for not telling him how low I'd come, I kept all those feelings of worthlessness to myself. Some people might think that to be prolific means a lack of artistic acumen. I wasn't about to correct them.

In October 1928, Daniel ambled in one time and joined us, and we gossiped freely about people we knew in the literary field, and about how the Yankees' "Murderers Row"—Ruth and Gehrig and the rest—had crushed the St. Louis Cardinals in the first game of the World Series that afternoon. After the stunning defeat of '26, when at the bottom of the ninth the Babe's attempted steal of second base gave the Series to St. Louis when Hornsby tagged him out, the Yanks were hot for a victory.

Mark, with tickets for the second game the next afternoon at Yankee Stadium, asked me and Daniel to join him. He was bringing the young son of a widow he had become acquainted with to the game. Although I was a diehard Giants fan, I wouldn't pass up the chance of going to a Series game, whoever was playing. It was a great day for New York, and I enjoyed the new friendships of these men.

Marie didn't serve liquor at her café. There were too many residents of the Washington Square area of the Village who didn't like her gypsy style and the Bohemian influence that was moving west toward the park, and they would have liked to see her and her artsy patrons gone. She wouldn't chance being shut down by the Feds, so she stuck with the nonalcoholic brews, which meant that if you wanted a beer or a stiff drink you had to find a speak. Late one night, at Mark's insistence for a more potent beverage, he sprung for drinks at Chumley's.

Chumley's, at 86 Bedford Street, cannot be seen from the street. We walked into a narrow alley between buildings that led into a small courtyard. Just ahead was an arched wooden door. Mark knocked and a square wooden panel slid to the side and an eye stared at us. It approved, I suppose, because a few moments later the door was unbolted and we were bid enter.

Chumley's opened a couple of years ago. Its proprietor is an Englishman with definite socialist leanings. I'd heard talk about its intellectual patronage, of course. Edmund Wilson and John Dos Passos, and men holding Marxist views frequent the place. It's been said to be a hotbed of sedition. I, knowing little about it, looked at my friends for elaboration. Daniel said that the Pen and Frog Society has regular meetings on the second floor, accessed through the dumbwaiter hidden behind the toiletry shelves in the ladies' room. He pointed to the ceiling and said, "That is where the plot to overthrow the United States government is always on the agenda."

Cleverly, the front for sedition is a speakeasy, another illegal venture, and although the police are not aware of the treasonous activities being conducted on the second floor, they are well aware of the variety of "tea" being served downstairs.

"Why, all a cop with a thirst for gin needs to do is stop in and ask for an "English tea," said Daniel. "If he prefers Seagram's 7, he just asks for "Canadian tea." The "Tennessee tea" will get you a Jack Daniels in a porcelain teacup. It's the real stuff, too!"

"But the serious stuff goes on upstairs and is unseen by the general public and the Feds," said Mark.

"Sounds like the kind of club kids make in hideouts," I said, but I didn't add that I grew up at the orphan asylum where such things were never a part of life.

"Yeah, secret handshake, coded messages," said Mark. "Ours was in the basement of a brownstone, Upper East Side, where the old woman we called the 'cat lady' squatted with her fifty cats."

"When we moved to the city from Newport when I was ten, I had no friends here. The neighborhood kids didn't like me, but when I found a construction shack that was left behind after they'd finished digging the subway near Ninetieth Street," laughed Daniel, "I had an idea. I told the boys that if they'd let me play with them, I'd get them a clubhouse. It took some engineering, but we hooked the shack up with chains, and a horse-cart dragged it through the yard to an empty lot behind a tenement house. I was a member of the gang, now."

"Your ingenuity paid off," I said.

"I felt like the king of the world. We covered it with brush and junk—anything we could find—to hide it."

"Our place smelled like cat piss, but it was our secret club," said Mark.

That's the night I learned more about Mark Wendt.

Born in '97, he was the only child of immigrant parents who lived on the Upper East Side, Ninety-Third Street, the Jewish neighborhood where the Marx Brothers grew up. His father was killed; he was a sandhog—drowned while on the job digging the East River section of the Pennsylvania Railroad tunnel. His mother waitressed to support them.

"I was a scrawny towhead, and a dreamer," he told me. A dreamer who, when lost in his fantasies, would wander across Lexington Avenue and get beaten up by the Irish kids, or by the German kids a few blocks south, "which was—still is—the way of the streets around town." He chuckled, "I always sported a shiner. Like a warrior's badge of courage.

"I wasn't like all the other neighborhood kids. I was small for my age, and kids made fun of me and pushed me around."

So he kept to himself and starting reading anything he could get his hands on.

"I hated school; the bullying was worse in the schoolyard. All I wanted to do was hide, escape. Reading was my escape."

Things changed when he approached puberty, and he shot up like a weed. It didn't make him many friends his own age, but the younger kids in his neighborhood gathered around him and he would tell them stories, mostly tales he'd made up himself, about knights and ladies and Arabian adventures.

It was discovered that he had a nice singing voice, and when he was twelve, he quit the sixth grade and joined a troupe of singers who performed for two-bits a night, a catfish dinner, and all the beer you could drink at an oyster joint on Forty-Sixth Street. There, he met Omar the Great, a down-and-out magician, a onetime headliner who sought comfort in a bottle after his wife and daughter were killed in a fire. Omar took a liking to the kid and taught him sleight-of-hand and card and coin tricks and several magic illusions, which Mark cleverly incorporated into a song-and-dance routine. It was novel enough to get him a featured spot at Harry's Harem, a nightclub frequented by theatricals and agents from the Albee Circuit. That's where he was seen by the casting agent for George M. Cohan's new show, *Hello, Broadway*, back in '14. So Mark Wendt began a career as a chorus boy in a string of shows. But what he did best was make up stories, which he began writing down. In '22 he got published. He's got eight books under his belt, all about the Wild West.

"Never been west of Jersey, but people eat that crap up," he said, in a self-deprecating manner.

He'd married a chorine, but she ran off with another guy years ago, before the books became popular and the money started rolling in. There were women, of course, since then. There would always be women who wanted Mark, I thought, but then he talked about Katie, a recently widowed young woman he knew, whose son, Bobby, he took to the ballgame. He was trying to help her, he said, had called an editor friend at Scribner's who was able to get her a job as a clerk. I thought, at first, it was because he, too, had been the only child of a widowed mother struggling to support her child, and he was doing a charitable act. But, as he spoke more and more about her, I saw a certain *something*, a change, the brightening of his eyes, emotion driving his words, and I knew he had more than a passing interest in the woman.

So the two things we three had in common was that we had shared the same publisher for a time, and we were all three single children who had suffered the loss of a father.

———◆———

It was to be a dismal winter for me. Harvey Price said he wasn't going to publish any more of my sex stories. Sex could be had easily these days, he said. It's everywhere you look when you walk down the street. "Free love," without inhibitions. Everybody under forty was doing it, talking about it. Sex was in vogue these days and the fashionable topic of public discussion. The Bright Young Things of today told each other all about their sex-lives. To shock was in style, and what better way to silence interfering parents than to talk about free love?

"Who needed to read about it when you could go out to a speak, get a girl tight, and fuck for free?" said Price.

Sex had gone mainstream in books, too, "if you could get a copy of that new book by D.H. Lawrence, *Lady Chatterley*, or that jerk-off tome, *Ulysses*," he added crudely.

So I had to take a job again, only now I wasn't a second-string drama critic; I was writing book reviews for ten bucks a pop for a magazine that I didn't think would last the year. And my lack of earning power made me uneasy when it came to Cherish.

Cherish, beautiful Cherish. . . .

We met in '24 at a cocktail party, and she approached me, famous author at the time, to say I had "the features of a ragged Titan prince." It was a double-edged compliment, and I laughed.

"Which one?"

"Man with a Glove," she said. "I fell in love with you at the Louvre."

The attraction was instant, heady, and powerful and we could not take our eyes off each other. By the next morning we lay exhausted in one another's arms.

Cherish, with the flame-red hair, my Bohemian woman of the past three years. The woman who first mistook me for a brilliant novelist; Cherish, who had been witness to my fall into a spiraling funk of depression. She knew little of my past. I dared not risk her knowing. I took the job to keep us going, until something better came along, or I could write something someone would publish.

I often wondered why she stayed with me, and when she would come to her senses and bolt out of my life. My greatest threat was Carlos Miguel Hernandez, the muralist, with whom Cherish shared a studio space in the attic of our apartment building.

Carlos Miguel is an earthy Mexican, handsome and charismatic. Dark, wide-set eyes, piercing with a smoldering intensity and set in a swarthy face, held magnetic attraction for women. His resonant voice rolled out to you with velvety, accented richness, ending consonants smoothed away like feathered brushstrokes. He used the attic studio as a place to store his paints, his tools for the trade, and to prepare huge stencils to outline his designs. He was out most of the day when working on one of his grand murals. His commissions were in the homes of the wealthy or adorning the walls of the lobbies of skyscrapers. And Cherish could be a compelling temptation to any man who glanced her way.

Part of her appeal, beyond her physical beauty, was that she spoke directly. Like a man to another man. Looked you right in the eye and spoke without the device of flirtation, the practiced feminine ploy to get a woman what she wants from a man. With Cherish there were no fluttering eyelashes, no demure smiles, no pretentions, just pure intent. This unconscious detachment had an appeal. Egos, especially those of powerful men, find that kind of romantic disinterest in a woman challenging. And Carlos, jovial, amiable, flashing a smile wider and whiter than snow-covered Alps on a sunny day, was a powerful man. Also, Carlos Miguel was an immensely likeable man. I felt small and puny next to his brawn. A faded, nondescript, pale, lanky, sandy-haired Jew from New York City with a past that made me leery of big, powerful, smiling men like Carlos. I tried to seize control of the green devil when it rose up inside me.

Sometimes, I thought she stayed with me only because she didn't have the heart to inflict the hurt that would surely come should she go. For Cherish had a heart as lovely and as graceful and as strong as her lithe body. Was it pity I saw when she gazed at me with those amazing eyes? Or was it empathy? I believed she loved me; a person without pretense cannot lie about these things. And she still believed in me when I had lost faith. How poor my life would be without her. I would never let her down, I promised myself each morning when I awoke in our cold flat above the shoemaker's shop.

Cherish found work for a time as an artist's model when she came to New York City five years ago. Her flawless white skin, blue eyes, and Botticelli nymph–like features graced the canvases of many post-romantics. But she was too ambitious to stand still for hours awaiting immortality through the brushstrokes of one or another of the many mediocre attempts to capture her soul. She decided she could do better. She had inherited a flare for things artistic, and her sketches were promising, so she was told, so she enrolled in art school while continuing to model to support herself. After her instructors told her she hadn't the talent to become a great painter like her father, who had been a traveling portrait painter of some repute, she gave it up. She never talked about her parents or her life before New York, and not wanting to return to the suburb of Cincinnati of her childhood, modeling remained her only option. She considered for a time the stage, but her heart wasn't in it, despite her beauty and the encouragement of admiring men for her to give it a go.

It happened one day, while walking to the studio of magazine illustrator Neysa McMein to pose for a cover of *Life*, that she watched a man pasting up a paper section of a billboard. Having recently discovered and been intrigued with the cubists and the new surrealism, she made a connection. The odd, random arrangement of colored paper laid atop an older image brought to mind a memory from her childhood: the figures of the Christmas crèche in her parents' house that had had a strange appeal to her. It had to do with the contrasting colors of the cheaply painted robes of the Virgin: a deep saturation of cerulean blue and turquoise. The colors infused her senses now, as they had back then. Those colors set side-by-side conjured emotions that she associated with the religious icon.

She told me that a sudden revelation flashed through her mind, an understanding she had not garnered from her time at the art academy: *color as imagery*. The laying on of color to tell a story and to evoke emotions.

Taking out her brushes and paints, she began to play with ideas for artworks blocking vivid color against unexpected contrasting color. After a while, she incorporated elements of the uncompleted billboard she had seen. Scraps of newsprint, partial phrases lending hints to a secret story buried beneath the new. A palimpsest of images to be deciphered by the discerning eye.

Soon she progressed to adding sculptural elements into these collages. She was repeating the imagery of the Virgin, she told me once, "with a blatant disregard for the purity and innocence of all that the Virgin represented, as is currently being expressed in our society."

She'd sold several works in as many months, enough for the rent and food, but not enough for us to beat the chill of poverty. So I would write the book reviews and try to find some other means of support. I decided to put aside my dream of writing the next Great American Novel.

And then, as if a curtain had been rung, Cherish, creator of the most outrageous abstract canvases, had received an unexpected visit to the attic studio this winter morning by a gallery owner, urged on by the ever-present Carlos, to see her work. Impressed, he promised her a show at his uptown gallery in the spring. She was becoming a success at last. Heartless as it sounds, I dreaded it.

I remember it happened in February 1929. By late afternoon the snow had begun, and in the darkness I fled the apartment to escape, not only the chill that seeped through the walls, but the cold prescience of the beginning of the end of my days with the woman I loved.

I was sitting near the woodstove at Romany Marie's, trying to beat off the terrible reality that I was despicably envious of my beloved's success, and awaiting the imminent loss of her love, when I felt a draft from the front door and looked up from my cup to see Mark stamping the snow off his boots and dusting off his fedora.

Despite his fairness, he looked deathly pale, his face drawn and his usual smile replaced by a stiff slash. I wondered if he had been ill. I hadn't seen him at the café since the New Year. At this time of day the café was nearly empty of customers, just me and a couple at a table across the room.

Mark caught my eye, and I could see a slight hesitation, a look of distress upon seeing me. The easy swagger I had come to expect was now a trudge toward my table. I wondered why he didn't immediately grab the chair to join me; instead, he stood before me, glassy-eyed and with a stunned expression.

Rising from my wallow in self-loathing, I said, "Sit down, Mark, you look beat!"

His eyes flitted around the room as if searching, weighing his options. Reluctantly, it seemed to me, he pulled out the chair and sat.

"You all right?" I asked, as Marie stepped out from the kitchen door. I caught her attention when she stopped short, as if sensing it best to keep her distance, and I motioned to bring a cup of coffee for Mark.

"You been sick?"

He didn't answer right away, just sat dumbly, staring at me with unseeing eyes. And then, holding my gaze, he whispered, more to himself than in reply to me, "She's dead."

He said no more, just the statement of fact, and his eyes never left my face.

Fancifully, I had the odd impression that I was the only thing on earth that he could latch onto, that grounded him, and that should he look away from me he would be inexorably thrown back into some hellish abyss and lost forever. I grabbed his arm. Marie brought the coffee and broke the spell. Sensing all was not well, she quickly retreated.

Mark's hands were red and chafed from cold and trembled as he made contact with the hot cup, and I knew he had meant Katherine Borso. Katie was dead.

"When?"

"Last night."

I could not think of anything to say that wouldn't have sounded trite. So we sat there, my silence ineffectual, his silence heavy with grief.

"I loved her, you know?" he finally said. "I wanted her, to marry her, you know?"

All I could do was nod and wait. But the silence had to be filled.

"Bobby?" I asked.

"With his dead father's sister in Brooklyn."

"How?"

"Car. Run down by a car. Crossing the street."

Mark's features collapsed into a grimace of pain, and he struck the table with his fist before saying, "Goddammit! She was running after Bobby."

"I don't—"

"Bobby dashed out," he said, and then looked at me. "I gave him a camera for his birthday. A Brownie. Showed him how to use it. Then he ran out to show the boys on the block, no coat. Katie called to him, but he kept going, so she . . . ran after him . . . and this car. I saw it happen . . . from the window."

"Oh, God, Mark!"

"It didn't stop. The bastard never stopped."

"But, that's—"

"She . . . died in my arms."

"Oh, God, Mark!"

"*I loved her!*" he blurted out with a desperate, wet choking. His eyes closed and his head dropped into waiting hands that gripped his hair.

And then, with a quiet resignation that was rife with loss, "We planned to marry in the spring."

"I'm sorry."

"Yes . . ."

"So sorry."

He stood up abruptly.

"What are you going to do, Mark?"

"I don't know."

"I mean, where are you going? Right now?"

"I don't know . . ."

"Stay. I mean, let's go get a drink," I said, as if I could afford a shot. Mark always had money, and if I had to spend the couple bucks I had in my pocket, I would. I couldn't let him wander around in the storm. Not tonight. Not like this. He had nowhere to go. I knew that he had no family. As successful as he was, the people he consorted with made for only casual and fleeting friendships. Publishing people were pretty much all business. Most writers were envious of their peers, especially successful ones, and Mark was successful. Show-people were always moving on; it is the nature of the business. I understood. Writers can live lonely lives.

Before this day, Mark and I were not really close, just friendly people who happened to patronize the same café. We admired each other for the gift we each thought we lacked and saw abundant in the other. I suppose it was his sudden expression of need that brought us together on more intimate terms.

I guided Mark to Chumley's, and after a couple of drinks to numb his senses, walked him home to his apartment. After getting him to bed, I went off to my own and the warmth of a newfound appreciation of the generous Cherish Winter.

Chapter Two

One evening about a month later, after recovering from a bout with the flu that had kept me apartment-bound for more than a week, I stopped into Marie's for her hot spiced tea, a brew that worked wonders to open my airways and relieve the sinus pressure, my nose being the bane of my existence and most affected by my illness. I had been for years a slave to nose-drops.

The place was busy, approaching dinner hour, and there was a rather animated group of young people—students, I guessed, from the university—gathered around, some seated, a few standing, an obviously fascinating personage hidden from my line of vision.

When there was raucous laughter and a sudden break in the huddle, I glimpsed the familiar face of Anthony Young, giving forth like the avuncular professor he was. When I heard his comment, "Murder is my specialty," he had my full attention. I took a table within earshot of the conversation—or to rephrase that—Anthony Young's learned observations.

Having entered the lecture late, I gleaned snatches that led me to understand it was all about a murder investigation he had read about in the newspapers, which had intrigued him. Most of the young people dispersed after a time, and it was then that Anthony spotted me. With a beaming smile of recognition he waved me over to join him, introducing me to the three remaining kids as the famous Ernest Stringer, author of *A Treasure of Tomorrows*, before drawing me into the conversation.

Anthony Young is a mystery writer who was met by a small success when he sent a manuscript of his first novel to Niles Pickering half-a-dozen years back, the first in a series featuring the fictional amateur detective, Professor Montague Fairchild, a paunchy, effeminate history professor who solves crimes by means of applying historical parallels to catch his criminals. One's first impression upon meeting Anthony is that he is the character of his own creation come to life, because Anthony is the personification of his fictional sleuth, a rather paunchy, effeminate history professor. Notwithstanding, the fifth mystery of his Professor Montague Fairchild series, *A Time to Reap*, is enjoying a third printing.

I already knew a lot about Young's background through newspaper interviews and the extended biographical page on the back cover of his books.

I knew that he was thirty-eight, born to Rose and Gerald Young in Minneapolis. His father, a stockbroker, moved the family, Anthony and a younger brother, to New York City after losing a pile in the Crash of 'Ninety-Three. Gerald, desperate to get back on his feet, took a job as an accountant with a Wall Street firm. Within ten years he had rebuilt his fortune. Anthony went off to prep school— Phillips Exeter Academy in New Hampshire—and graduated from Princeton after switching his major from business to Greco-Roman Studies. There was some contention from his father, who had expected him to join the brokerage house he'd established in 1900.

After graduation, Anthony did the European tour, spent a summer in Greece, and came home before the war in Europe broke out. He went on to short-term professorships at several small New England colleges, teaching the classics. I was to learn that he had yet to marry and has no known children. From the way he talks and brazenly flirts with women, I got the impression that he fancies himself a ladies' man, although there is a slight, if at times disturbing, effeminacy about him in his gestures and flamboyant speech. I've run across notices in the newspapers announcing his lectures on classical literature and the Greek tragedians, presented at various women's clubs and civic organizations. I was curious to know more about him, but to ask about his life story might be intrusive. Anyway, I enjoy the slow reveal while getting to know someone. Through casual conversation, I would later find out that he was a master at bridge, could pilot an aeroplane, and had memberships at various men's clubs around town. When his parents died in a car crash while vacationing in Paris in '24, he inherited the firm and a small fortune.

This sudden financial independence allowed him the leisure to travel, and after a year of the grand world tour he decided that now he could fulfill the youthful dream of novel writing. It was then that he embarked on a career as a mystery writer.

"When writing a mystery plot," expounded Young, "you try to depict the perfectly executed premeditated crime. This makes for a clever protagonist and gives your detective a real challenge. The detective must find the one overlooked detail that will bring down the culprit. There is always some little thing that goes wrong in the execution of a crime."

I had to smile at his fervent instruction. I could see he was really passionate about his subject.

"To paraphrase Dostoyevsky's Raskolnikov in *Crime and Punishment*: 'A criminal is caught because at the time of his crime he loses the ability to reason.' You see, the criminal cannot predict the loss of a shirt button, the shedding of coat fibers, the passerby who sees his face when leaving the scene of the crime. It's the little unexpected things that may give one away, no matter how perfectly one plans the execution of a crime."

When the other students had departed, Anthony Young was about to order dinner and asked me to be his guest. I accepted and we continued our discussion.

"Well, I haven't read many mysteries," I admitted. "But, yes, Dostoevsky's *Crime and Punishment* . . . and, oh, yes, I read *The Lodger*—"

"Yes, of course," said Young. "Marie Belloc Lowndes."

"And Simenon's stories—"

"He's was a crime reporter, you know," said Young.

"I didn't know."

"That young man is a marvel. Why, he can put out forty, fifty, sixty pages a day. When I met Georges at the Café de Flores, not so long ago, he told me about a book he was commissioned to write. His character was to be a detective and he was trying to decide what name to give him. I suggested Maigret— Commissionaire Maigret. I thought it humorous that such a prolific writer would struggle for so long over what to name his protagonist."

"Is Simenon really that prolific?" I asked, disbelieving it possible.

"Oh, God, yes, and it's good stuff, too! It just rolls out onto the page. He puts us all to shame," he chuckled.

"What you said about Dostoyevsky . . . about the criminal losing the ability to reason . . ."

Anthony Young waited patiently, smilingly, for the question that would follow my preface. "What I mean is," I said, trying to form my words as an idea took form in my head, "what if you write a book where the culprit gets away with his crime, as I'm sure happens all the time?"

I was thinking about Mark and the hit-and-run death of his beloved Katie. As far as I had heard almost two weeks ago, before falling ill with the flu, an arrest had not yet been made. In fact, the car that had struck Katie down before fleeing had not been identified, although Mark witnessed the incident and remembered the make and model. Several eyewitnesses also noted details about the car. There just was not enough evidence to make an arrest as yet; there were denials and a firm alibi for one possible suspect who owned a car that matched the description. It belonged to a wealthy gent, Simon Strong, whose estate on the Long Island Sound was believed to have been purchased with a bootlegging fortune. Mark voiced his despair that the bastard would get away with his crime.

Anthony Young considered his reply, and then said, "Readers want vindication; they want a resolution; they want the criminal caught. And they want him properly punished. There are perfect murders committed every day that are mistaken as accidents, suicides, illnesses. Real life has to take a backseat in popular fiction."

"But," I continued, "don't you think that if, at story's end, the reader is privy to the identity of the criminal and the ending is open to the *possibility* that the villain will eventually be caught and punished for his crime through some blemish in his nature—"

"The Greek tragedian's *fatal flaw*?"

"Yes, *that* will do him in."

"Shakespeare used that device over and over again—that an innate flaw in character will eventually lead to a criminal's downfall."

"Yes," I said, "and so, after the reader has closed the cover of the book, he would find vindication and not be disappointed."

"*Hmmm*," said Anthony Young, nodding as he considered the idea. "But, Shakespeare *included* the downfall. None of his villains get away with their crimes. They all die before the curtain falls on the play. The vindication. And yet, you have a point . . . I suspect . . . with the right publisher, I suppose . . . a book like that—one depicting the perfect crime— well, it could get banned as immoral in Boston and make a big splash and prove you right."

"You think so?"

"But it won't *satisfy*."

When we had finished our lamb stew and drunk the last of our coffee we walked out into the cold night. A drizzle of freezing rain had formed misty orbs around the hot streetlamps. The sheen of ice on the cobblestones faded away when a breath of steam eerily rose from a manhole cover like a genie escaping his lamp.

There was no foot traffic, and only the occasional vehicle passing through the intersection a hundred feet north. The air was redolent with the mingling odors of the river at low tide, rancid cooking oil, and ever-present automobile exhaust fumes. I pulled my cap down and raised my coat collar against the damp.

Anthony tucked his cashmere scarf deeper under his coat and looked out from under his Borsalino to peer into the darkened storefront windows of the three-story brick buildings lining the narrow street, as if deciding, *what next?*

He pulled on his gloves and then flexed his fingers. "Scotch over at Rusty's?"

He didn't wait for my reply, just led the way toward the intersection.

It was that night, with Anthony Young and engaging in the discussion of the mystery genre, that I became intrigued with the idea of authoring my own mystery story. With a mystery, I could devise a very plausible puzzle to be solved—a plot of my own device, of course, but one that my characters would have to systematically solve along with the reader. I could entangle these puzzle-solvers with *red herrings*, as Anthony had explained were false or inconsequential clues, and assign alibis, some true, some contrived, one misleading, revealing facts in a timely way. After that, all I'd need to do is create a few interesting characters and a fascinating protagonist. I was soon to discover that there was infinitely more required for making a good mystery soup than throwing together a bunch of ingredients.

My initial enthusiasm and belief that the process was a cinch to accomplish was dampened the next week when I met Anthony once again at Marie's, and he spoke of the psychological aspects that drive people toward murder: motives. Then I understood something that many writers never get, or refuse to understand: You *can* write a great book, one that is compellingly real and *true*, emotionally as well as psychologically true, with a plot that moves in a lineal fashion toward discovery! It had to do with timing, character building, and much more than simple puzzle solving.

When he asked if I had read Theodore Dreiser's book, published last year, *An American Tragedy*, and I said that I had not, I received in the mail the next day a copy of it from Anthony with a note stating: *Sometimes the greatest works of fiction are steeped in mystery and teeming with crime.*

It was very late, and while we drank in a darkish corner of the near-empty speak, in walked Stephen Shaw accompanied by Trevor Hunter. Shaw saw us and, wanting nothing to do with us, threw a savage look our way. I could see his obvious contempt for Anthony as he sidled up to the bar.

Hunter I knew casually. I'd seen him at Marie's having dinner with Bucky Fuller, who I always thought was a pretentious prick who took advantage of the café proprietress with his costly and ridiculous decorations of her place, which had to go, finally, because of their lack of functionality. I didn't think Fuller, who projected the image of the "great artiste," deserved the free meals he was fed there. So, because of my dislike for Bucky Fuller, I'd had nothing much to do with his friend, Trevor Hunter.

It was publishing industry gossip that nobody would touch Stephen Shaw after mobsters threatened Niles Pickering for publishing Shaw's exposé on the world of sanitation. Stephen Shaw is a real rabble-rouser, who, rather than beating down prejudice and corruption as Upton Sinclair has tried to do through his brilliant exposés, only manages to incite violent emotions. His books are carelessly researched, and more than once he has been sued for defamation. He successfully manipulates faction against faction, and hasn't a decent thing to say about Jews, Negros, or Italians. He purports to support Labor; he is a communist who rails against anarchism and socialism even though they are all waging the same fight for the worker. Beefy, brawny, pock-faced, Shaw is a wily ginger-haired devil with a big mouth stamped with a smirk that brings to mind a scheming Iago. If it weren't for his cunning, I'd think him a fool. People like Shaw often have nasty agendas. But you don't always know what they are.

When Hunter caught sight of us he came over to say hello. I suspected that as Anthony Young and I were in deep philosophical discussion, what Hunter really wanted to do was find out what we were talking about. Any amusement would have trumped Shaw's blathering political tirades. They were an odd couple, Shaw and Hunter: the rabble-rouser and the sophisticated intellectual.

In spite of his association with Buckminster Fuller and now Shaw, I didn't really know the man; he always struck me as a dark soul, an impression fostered by the thick black brows that dominated his face.

What strikes one upon first meeting Hunter are those eyebrows. Positioned far below a high dome, they are strikingly expressive and black and silky, and the high, white forehead suggests a superior intellect. I fancied those eyebrows to be Russian sable pelts pinned above his lashless gray eyes. A nervous twitch on his sallow left cheek occasionally sets the left brow aquiver, which is unsettling, to say the least, for it gives the impression that one furry critter is not quite dead and is struggling to escape. It conveys a menacing impression. And because of a war injury to his left leg, he walks with a slight limp.

So much about Hunter was unsettling for me. My prejudice was solely founded on appearance, of course, because he has authored several fine volumes in which he psychologically profiles real-life criminals and their victims. One might say he is a Renaissance man: a criminologist, botanist, and forensic scientist on the cutting edge of new discoveries. Hunter was a thoroughbred in the stable of Niles Pickering.

I was soon to learn that his face didn't depict the man very accurately. I was to learn from Anthony that he knew Hunter quite well. Hunter's affiliation as a student of Arthur Conan Doyle prompted Niles Pickering to suggest that Anthony Young consult Hunter on occasion when researching his mystery novels. I learned sometime later that Hunter was quite generous with his knowledge of forensic science. And this association eventually fostered a friendship. It was Hunter who taught Young how to fly an aeroplane, a hobby that was to become a great passion for him, and it was Young who oversaw the magnificent renovation of the dreary townhouse off Fifth Avenue that Hunter inherited after his father's death.

Shaw, left at the bar and having imbibed too much over the course of the evening—he was quite drunk—bounded over toward us, his nose out of joint, obviously slighted at Hunter's abandonment. He carried his effrontery over to our table.

Hunter bought a round of drinks and managed to placate Shaw with outrageous comments alluding to Shaw's genius. I quickly picked up on what Hunter was doing: It was an effort to defuse Shaw. I wondered why Hunter even bothered to seek out the companionship of such a brutish character. I later found out they had met earlier in the evening at a Chinatown opium den.

Hunter was well aware of Shaw's paranoia and his confrontational nature. Once, I watched as Shaw accused a speakeasy bartender, fifty feet across a room, of talking derisively about him to a girl sitting at the bar with her fiancé. The bartender had never seen Shaw before in his life, and was surprised when the brawny bear suddenly bolted at him full-speed from across the room to leap the bar and pummel him mercilessly before a dozen men pulled him off.

I can't say exactly at which moment our discussion suddenly shifted from Shaw's recitation of his numerous complaints—from those on the grand scale of American politics on down to his own petty personal gripes, real or imagined—but suddenly the four of us were engaged in a discourse on revenge.

Hunter cited references in the Hebrew Bible to "an eye for an eye" as not meant to be taken literally, according to rabbinic teachings; rather such injuries demand monetary compensation equal to the value of the loss. "Do not seek revenge." "Love your neighbor as yourself." *Forgiveness* of indiscretions, of injuries inflicted, is the goal of Man, as "Vengeance is mine, sayeth the Lord."

Young spoke of seeking vengeance as the great theme in literature, of the affinity for revenge in Greek Tragedy, from the extremes of Medea's madness to Hamlet seeking retribution for his father's murder, to Othello's betrayal for his jealous rage, even to the horror of Poe's stories.

"There are those I could kill," said Shaw, nodding slowly, teeth bared. I saw the glint of his steely eyes in the darkish room and imagined he was choosing his victims right at that moment, and that Anthony Young was at the top of his list. The zeal with which he spoke held a vile intent and sent a shiver through me. Was he putting us on? I remember thinking that if ever there was a man who would kill for the thrill of it, it was Shaw.

Making light of his remark, I said, "How would you do the deed? A poisoned coronet like Medea, or a stab in the back?"

Anthony Young spit out a hollow laugh. "The first is more efficient, the second far too bloody."

Shaw leaned his big chest across the table and brought his dark face close to Anthony's and hissed through a grimace of delight, "Ah, but spilt blood is so much more satisfying."

"Poison is for the faint at heart, I suppose," said Anthony, trying to recover from Shaw's scrutiny. A heavy odor wafted across the table of stale whiskey, spent tobacco, traces of opium smoke, and unwashed flesh, accosting Shaw's antithesis, the fixatedly tidy professor.

Anthony rose from the table and nervously set about retrieving his coat and hat, fished some money from his billfold and placed the bills down before me, babbling words to the effect that it was very late and there were appointments in the morning, and so on, and then strode quickly out of the speak.

Shaw sat back wearing a self-satisfied grin, having properly unnerved Anthony Young. His behavior had further sunk my previously low estimation of him. He had brazenly pushed his way into our discussion, hijacked it, and before very long had become its critic.

After some minutes Hunter left to go home for the night, and, not wanting to be left alone with Shaw, I, too, rose to walk home through a flurry of snow. I feared that Shaw might try to catch up with me, but when I turned to look back over my shoulder he was talking animatedly with Hunter as the two passed under the light of a streetlamp a block distant.

I was glad of the time I had earlier, getting to know a little bit more about Anthony Young. He was not at all as I had perceived him. I found Anthony to be a charming raconteur, very learned and far more astute than his mystery series suggested. The rather prissy effeteness Anthony presented to the world seemed to melt away in the light of his kindness and intelligence. We were so very different from one another. The faces we presented to the world were in sharp contrast: I, a bit scruffy and intense, he, meticulous and lighthearted. I was the pessimist, he, the optimist. I liked the man tremendously, and it was mutual, I believe. I wished in many ways to be more like him, to emulate his self-confidence, and to emulate the good fellowship he naturally projected.

Anthony appeared to admire my dedication to the literary arts and my ambition to write a good book.

After some time getting to know him, I even began to believe in his confidence that I would one day achieve my goals. This is a rare thing to be had from another author, in a business that is cutthroat and dollar driven, and a great gift from one as successful as he. It raised a newborn confidence in me that was heady and inspiring and renewed my hope for the future.

As for Trevor Hunter, he was a surprise to me as well.

He, too, was a considerate man, generous in nature, and not at all what his countenance initially suggested him to be. He wasn't judgmental; he was an observer of personalities, and his intellectual pursuits rose above petty grievances. Because he was so comfortable in his own skin it was not unusual for him to engage with men like Bucky Fuller and Stephen Shaw. Still, I wondered if he had ever known anyone on a really intimate level.

The next afternoon, I was walking down Sixth Avenue when I saw Mark standing in a doorway. He looked like a ghost of himself, and far thinner than when we last saw each other at Marie's the month before. I did a double-take as I was passing him, and at the second look he nodded, confirming it was really him. I wondered, when was the last time he'd had a decent meal?

"I've tried telephoning, Mark, but there's never any answer."

"I've been out a lot."

"What's been going on?"

There was a nervous energy about him in the way he slipped the silver dollar through his fingers, faster and faster, like a samurai juggling his sword and ready for an attack.

I did not want to ask about developments in the case against the hit-and-run driver responsible for Katie's death, but given the state he was in, it was probably the only thing on his mind. I asked about his health, to which he replied, "Really, Stringer, do you need to ask?"

"All right, you look like shit, Mark," I blurted, suddenly frightened for him.

"Thanks for noticing."

"What are you doing here?" I asked, and when he didn't answer, "Got time for a cup of coffee?" indicating the automat across the avenue.

"Can't," he said, looking past me and across the street as if waiting for something to happen there. "Got to stay put here."

"Meet me at Marie's later?"

"I—probably not tonight. I have things to do."

Mark turned to look at me, and his eyes scrutinized mine. In the searching look there was an urgent appeal. I got the strange feeling he had forgotten who I was.

He smiled patiently, "Aren't you going to ask me about Katie and her killer and all the crap the cops are telling me? That's what you want to know, isn't it?"

"What are you saying? That the cops are in cahoots with—"

"Money washes away witnesses' memories and greases palms, Stringer."

"Well, what can you do?" I asked.

"I get the bastard."

"Mark!"

"Oh, don't get all nuts on me. I didn't buy a gun or anything. I just want to trap the bastard."

"How?" I asked.

"If I can get him to admit what he did . . ."

"How will you do that?" I asked. "What makes you think—?"

"I don't know! I kidnap him, beat the crap out of him, and when I'm through he'll beg to tell the truth."

"And you go to jail," I said. "Great plan."

"I won't go to jail."

"Oh, no?"

"*Nah*. They'd find me dead first. You got a better idea?"

"No. But do try to devise a way to get him to confess that won't get you jailed for fifty years."

I had barely finished speaking when out from a speakeasy across the street walked Simon Strong, accompanied by two men.

Simon Strong, in his late fifties and wearing the majority of his bulk around his waist, was dressed as any self-respecting so-called financier would have been expected to dress, only everyone knew he was a bootlegger running rum out from the Long Island Sound. He wore a pearl-gray vested suit, below which spats peeked out over Italian leather shoes. The diamond stud tie pin flashed wealth in the sunlight. His dark-gray mink-trimmed overcoat rested casually over his shoulders.

Mark pocketed the coin, his rapt attention now on Strong, walking stick under his arm, placing his hat atop his dark, slicked-back hair, and pulling on gloves. The three walked a short distance up the avenue and got into a parked Duesenberg.

After they'd driven off, Mark's attention turned toward me. It was in that moment that I knew for sure that it was Simon Strong had run down Katie.

Mark said, "What do you think of this plot?"

"What do you mean?" I asked, as the car turned off the avenue. I looked into bloodshot eyes.

"For a new book?"

His eyes widened, and I could tell that his plot had nothing to do with a book.

"Want to pass it by me?" I asked.

He hesitated while scrutinizing my face as if evaluating his confidence in me. "Not yet," he said, with an expression of warning that made me think he might be planning something terrible, suicide, perhaps. "I'm still working out the kinks."

"You need to find a way," I said ineffectually.

I knew there was nothing I could do to help Mark bring Katie's killer to justice. I just wanted him to know that I understood his loss, without revealing my own miserable past. He looked so vulnerable, so raw, and so fiercely calm. His passion for revenge was greater than any sense of self-preservation and I feared the consequences should he take matters into his own hands.

My concern must have shown in my face, because he looked at me with amusement in his eyes. I opened my mouth to deliver a gentle warning, but before I could speak, Mark walked off without another word.

A few days later, while riding the El uptown, I picked up a discarded copy of the *Daily News* from off the seat, and while perusing its pages, a familiar name caught my eye on the Society page. Among the passengers on the manifest who had departed on the midnight crossing of the Mauritania was the Wall Street financier Simon Strong and his wife, Helena. And then I received a note in the post from Mark that afternoon apologizing for his rudeness when we'd met on the street, and telling me that he was leaving town on a trip to California. Sam Goldwyn had beckoned. Hollywoodland was calling. There was interest in making a motion picture of one of his cowboy books! By the time I got his note, he said, he'd be somewhere near Chicago on the Twentieth Century. He'd be gone for a month and hoped the California sunshine would prove restorative. I felt relieved.

Mark and Daniel knew about Anthony Young and his kind tutelage in my desire to write a mystery novel. Mark thought it a good idea, and was considering writing one himself. He'd been thinking about making his protagonist a detective on the murder squad, a man grappling with graft and corruption. It was to be a hardboiled and dark depiction of city life. I was enthusiastic about his vision and with his popularity among his male readership it would be a surefire bestseller.

And so, when Mark returned from California and met Daniel and me at Marie's, I reminded him about our talk, about wanting to write a crime novel.

Daniel listened for a bit, and then said, "You know, I think I need a plan, boys. A plan to write within the constraints of what is called these days a 'genre.' Maybe mystery writing is the way."

I talked more about Anthony Young and suggested they meet him to discuss and share his knowledge of the unique process of writing such books.

Anthony was flattered when I asked him to talk with us. He appeared to relish his role as teacher. He asked if we'd mind if he brought Trevor Hunter to the meeting. I knew I was answering for Mark and Daniel when I said, "Of course," but

I didn't see why there'd be a reasonable objection. The request proved to me that Young was quite free of professional envy by inviting Hunter to share with the young writers his insights as well. Daniel—who saw all fellow writers as potential plagiarists—hit the morgue at the *Saturday Evening Post* to research Hunter before trusting his new ideas with a stranger who might steal his next novel. He shared with me and Mark what he had found out.

"Trevor Hunter is singularly strange."

"As if that's news," I said.

"Did you know he was born to a fortune? He's considered somewhat of a genius; fiddles around with his rarified intellectual pursuits, but hasn't written anything really original," prefaced Daniel.

"Do you refute the man's genius?" I asked, annoyed with Daniel's sour assessment.

He pursed his lips in annoyance, and consulted his little pocket notebook.

"Trevor Hunter. He is a very peculiar one," he nodded. "Supposedly has a half-dozen books in the works—or short stories, I don't know."

"More than I'm doing," I said.

"His maternal grandfather, a Canadian named Samuel Spencer, was a snake-oil salesman back before the War Between the States, who later concocted a tonic for dyspepsia, which supposedly worked. Daddy made a fortune when a British pharmaceutical company, Peabody-Hunter, bought the formula. You remember Cocana Cure?"

"Yeah," I said, remembering the blue bottle sitting on the shelf in the bathroom of my aunt's and uncle's apartment. "My uncle used to guzzle it."

"Right, well, Samuel Spencer's daughter, Margaret, fell in love with and married the pharmaceutical owner's son and heir, Victor Hunter, and after they had taken up residence in London, Margaret gave birth to a son, Trevor. Two other siblings followed, both dead, now, Spanish influenza."

"That explains his vast knowledge of drugs," I said.

"After a fine public school education, young Trevor went on to Oxford. A botanist. He became an expert mycologist."

"What's—" asked Mark.

"Mushrooms. I had to look it up."

"Royal Air Force, he flew twenty missions before he was shot down. Leg got it bad."

"That accounts for the limp," I said.

"When Trevor inherited his father's company in 'Twenty-one, he sold it and moved to the States. Everyone thinks he's a genius—"

"Well, isn't he?" I said.

"*Awww*, delusions of grandeur! And he claims a friendship with Sir Arthur Conan Doyle."

"Well, is he or isn't he a friend?" asked Mark.

"Well, yes. Doyle is his godfather," said Daniel.

"So what you alluded to as suspect is actually true," I said in Hunter's defense.

"Yes, all right. He has a connection to Doyle."

"Anything more," I asked Daniel, "other than the fact that you already dislike the fellow before ever meeting him?"

Daniel flashed me a sour look before ending in a disparaging tone: "Never married, not much interest in long-term relationships with women, but he manages to seduce plenty, and is especially attracted to the married ones."

I was about to make a crass locker-room remark about women in general, when Daniel added the last bit of information like an exclamation point, hoping to turn us against the fellow: "And he is an opium fiend!"

"Well, that ruins him for me," said Mark, rolling his eyes and feigning disdain.

I stifled a chuckle.

As the Conan Doyle apostolate was the next best thing to Doyle himself, and because I didn't like Daniel's allusions to the man's character, I warmly welcomed Trevor Hunter when he arrived at Marie's with Anthony. And to throw Daniel even further off his game of bashing the learned and accomplished man, Hunter was quite candid and forthcoming, offering his vast knowledge of drugs and forensics to better our story plots.

As I was soon to learn, Hunter was a walking reference library in the field of criminology. We engaged in a short and enthusiastic discourse, and then, as the evening progressed and the noise of the café became intolerable for conversation, Anthony suggested we continue our talk in the comfort of his Washington Square row house to pursue further the creation of the perfect murder plot.

And so our get-togethers continued over the next few months. We'd meet for dinner at Marie's and then we'd walk over to Anthony's house for drinks and continued conversation, Hunter telling us about murder cases he had probed into, and the capture of murderous criminals throughout the annals of history. We were scouts huddled around a campfire, listening to macabre tales of horror, while Anthony stoked the logs in his fireplace. We would freely, trustingly discuss ideas for plots. Cousins was always reticent; convinced of having been plagiarized in the past, he couldn't risk it in his future. But because he was very astute, Daniel offered the occasional suggestion for untangling the unexpected snags in everyone else's plot scenarios.

On a blustery night in April 1929, we were asked to forgo our preliminary meeting at Marie's to spend the entire evening at Anthony's. It being his birthday, he had his cook prepare a sumptuous supper of rack of lamb in celebration of his forty-ninth year. By ten o'clock, a mixture of snow and sleet had iced the Village sidewalks and paths through Washington Square, making foot passage treacherous. Looking out from the curtained windows I saw that the imminently budding rain-trees in the park were encased in sleeves of ice, glittering in the light of the park lamps and the spots lighting the great arch. The park at night takes on a strange aspect. On foggy nights people have witnessed the ghosts of the dead rising from beneath the old potter's field; those who died from Yellow Fever walk in yellow-stained shrouds; those hung from the long-gone great elm float by with elongated necks. Some say it is fancy, but I know the dead walk among us. They follow us, they can haunt us all of our lives.

I was called back to the land of the living, to the comfort of the lovely drawing room, at the sound of Anthony's voice. Premium Scotch, "just off the boat" and delivered by Anthony's bootlegger, was poured, and we settled deep into the big cushy chairs and sofas facing the crackling fire.

We were about to get a lesson from Trevor Hunter on the selection of the appropriate poisons to be used by our various murderous characters in our respective murder mystery novels.

Not all "green deaths" were equal, he told us. Some botanicals were harder to procure than others, or had to be processed in such a way that they would release their lethal qualities. Trevor, son of a pharmaceutical heir and a botanist himself, gave us a brief history of poisons, from where they derived, and a list of notorious users. Mark, Daniel, and I were enthralled. Anthony stated that "there was always something new to learn about this sort of weaponry."

"Poisons are weapons, aren't they?" murmured Daniel.

"Oh, yes!" said Anthony. "Why it's like choosing the right gun—a pistol, shotgun, revolver?—to do the job right!"

"Why not the gun?" asked Mark. "Makes short work to resolve a big problem."

"Too easy, I should say," said Anthony. "And with the new ballistics testing, pointing an accusing finger to the owner of the gun, too easy to get caught."

Mark was about to protest when Trevor jumped in:

"I know, I know!" He used his pipe for emphasis. "Guns are a handy weapon, especially in the Wild West, as seen in your book series, Mark, but they are the stuff of cowboys and gangsters, and the occasional gun moll who wants to rub out an abusive husband or lover."

"It's gaining in popularity, especially in Chicago," said Anthony, referring to the murder trials of Belva Gaertner and Beulah Annon.

"I see you are up to date on popular culture, Tony," said Trevor, feigning surprise.

"Well, it intrigued me, this new trend to shoot first and then admit to the crime with the defense of 'he made me do it.'"

"The onus on the dead man," nodded Trevor. "Still, it is the means to an end employed by the lower classes. It has no . . ."

"Glamour?"

"Yes, Trevor, that's it."

"But these women, albeit of the lower classes, were glamorous enough to have a play written about them," I said.

"*Chicago*, yes," nodded Trevor. "Thanks to the profane appeal for nationwide news coverage, it proved a comedy of errors, I should say! But let us talk about poisons, the murder weapons of kings and queens."

Anthony sat down on the sofa and gave the floor to his friend.

"Let me tell you the story of Cleopatra, and how she came to choose her poison."

Mark chuckled and said, "Trevor, you speak as gaily as if the Egyptian Queen were deciding which wallpaper should cover her palace walls."

Trevor's eyes widened.

"*Ha-ha!*" he rang out with a startling yelp. "*Wallpaper!*"

"What did I say?" asked Mark.

"*Wallpaper*, the cause of many accidental poisonings during the last century!"

"You caused a short detour, Mark," said Anthony. "Wallpaper can wait, Trevor."

Mark said, "You were talking about Cleopatra?"

Trevor nodded, packing his pipe with tobacco.

"Yes, Cleopatra. . . . She was devastated by the death of Marc Anthony, and feared capture by Octavius. She probably would have preferred feigning death, but unlike Shakespeare's Juliet, there were no such brews. So suicide was her only option. The means, however, were numerous.

"Not wanting to die a grotesque death, she commissioned her physician to procure a number of poisons and to have them administered to slaves and prisoners so that she might observe the processes of each death. Laurel water—a cyanide drink, hemlock, arsenic, and quicksilver—liquid mercury. All resulted in horrible and disfiguring deaths.

"Determined, she suggested the asp—but her physician told her it was not a pleasant death and that the cobra bite would result in physical distortion. Still, a cobra was smuggled into her bedchamber in a basket of figs, and Cleopatra ended her life by the fangs of the cobra."

"So, if we can't get our hands on a cobra, and we are looking for a graceful end to our troubles, what else is there?" I asked.

"We want what is easy to procure, of course. There's arsenic. Pure arsenic is Number 33 on the Periodic Table. It is rarely seen in its pure form because, while still in the earth, it likes to adhere to an array of other minerals. It burns off through the smelting process, and changes color according to its host minerals. Add sulphur, it's a bright yellow; add iodine, it appears red; with a bit of copper and potash it is rendered a lovely blue!"

"Wallpaper, Trevor?" said Anthony.

"Ah, yes, I digress. The most potent, most lethal form of arsenic is the gas produced, called *arsine*. It occurs when metals such as zinc are treated with hydrochloric acid. Go back half a century and you will hear that the beautiful papers that graced the walls of many fine homes used arsenic to produce the vibrant colors for their designs. When bacteria attacked the surfaces, this lethal gas, arsine, was released. It is quite toxic and there is no known antidote. Why, an American ambassador in Italy died as he slept in his bed surrounded by four walls of capricious foliage.

"As we are on the subject of arsenic," Trevor continued, "let me say that it has been used for centuries, not as a poison, but as a remedy for asthma, treating sores, and aborting 'obstructions,' as women liked to refer to unwanted pregnancies. It has been used to treat syphilis—Gustav Flaubert found it useful, personally, to treat his disease as well as for filling the mouth of his tragic heroine, Emma Bovary. It was hailed as a skin whitener for Elizabeth I and centuries of women after her; women fed it to their husbands for its aphrodisiacal effects, because in small doses it produces sexual excitability. The Greek term, *arsenikon,* does, after all, mean *potent*. Its enthusiasts, known as *arsenophagists,* chewed lumps of it. Added to horses' feed, it glistens the coat and keeps the animal conditioned and spirited.

"Last century it was the rat poison of choice, especially popular with women hoping to rid their household of four-footed rats as well as the two-legged variety. Inheritor's choice—how better to finish off tight-fisted Uncle Harold who turned eighty and was determined to live another twenty years?

"The problem with arsenic is that it is detectable—first through its symptoms and then after death, thanks to modern methods of postmortem testing. But if administered in small doses over a long period of time, added to the dinner plate, mixed in beverages, it mimics several diseases. The fatal dose ends the misery. Keep in mind that its preparation within a household is best done in the kitchen, and often is the cause of entire families risking acute sickness if not death. And as a woman's place is in the kitchen, it became the choice of many unhappy wives."

"I don't like using arsenic in my mysteries, Trevor," said Anthony. "It's a long haul, and frankly, it's old hat."

"Right you are, dear Tony!" said Trevor with a bounce in his step as he struck a long fireplace match to light his briar pipe. "Fast-acting poison is usually the best."

"But not so fast that the murderer cannot remove himself from the scene before it takes effect," said Anthony.

"Yes, that is a great consideration. . . . Strychnine is easily obtained from the chemist's shop, and like arsenic was used last century as an aphrodisiac as well as an appetite booster. It reeks, though, and even diluted has a bitter taste. It's a paralytic, attacking first the spinal cord and then the cortex of the brain. It is a five-part death, although death may occur at any of the first stages when the body convulses, appears to recover for a time, and then the convulsions repeat. It is not a pretty death."

"I prefer cyanide," said Anthony, refilling his glass.

"Do you, now . . . ?" Trevor said, as if they were talking about their preferences for shirt collars.

"Poison of choice?" chuckled Mark.

"What?" asked Anthony, distracted momentarily. "Oh! Yes, I see what you mean, Mark. Actually, cyanide is pretty fast acting, depending on how it is administered. From a few seconds to up to three hours. Smoke a cigarette laced with cyanide, and the fumes kill you within a minute. Ingestion may slow the process, but if absorbed through the mucous membranes, like the suicide capsule, or through a cut or abrasion, the results will lead to a quick death. So, you see, the murderer can pretty much decide on the approximate time of death, and be far from the scene of the crime before his victim expires."

"Thallium, Anthony, thallium!" said Trevor, gleefully, cupping the bowl of his pipe, and bobbing it for effect. He stepped away from the mantel. "Thallium is a *marvelous* poison!"

I had to laugh at their excited exchange. One might have expected such enthusiasm after sampling a fine vintage.

"Except, Trevor, there is hair loss, as you told me when I was choosing my poison for my last book."

"How better to eliminate an old, bedridden, *bald* geezer than with daily applications of a thallium-tainted ointment on his bedsores?"

"'Poor nurse,' I remember you saying."

"On further consideration I remembered that medical people wear rubber gloves for such things."

"You suggested I choose digitalis."

"That's right; causes heart failure," nodded Trevor. "No one would suspect anything other than a heart attack."

I listened as Mark asked a few questions about the availability of such deadly potions, and the ease of an ordinary person obtaining them. I was struck with a sense of the macabre during this exchange, the cavalier responses; despite the waves of heat emanating from the fire, I shivered from the proverbial footsteps treading on my grave.

How to kill someone. . . .

Having witnessed the brutal murder of my mother, I suppose I was especially sensitive to the diabolical nature of the talk. But then, who wouldn't be appalled?

I tamped down my squeamishness.

Looking back, I think I was attracted, as well as repelled, by the subject of violence and murder.

I supposed talking and writing about it would be cathartic, and a way of purging my innermost fears. After all, the crime scenes were imaginary. Being the son of a murderer, I had wondered if there was murder in my heart, by way of inheritance. My weak stomach for the topic fared better when I told myself that we were discussing the use of these drugs to kill someone, not in real life, but in a murder mystery novel.

Overall, I came to enjoy these sessions spanning the elements to consider in the creation of the mystery novel. Daniel began writing again, and Mark seemed to rally after his long winter of despair. By the end of May I had begun to plot a story, but with the distraction of Cherish's show about to open at the uptown gallery, I put those ideas aside. Money was on my mind, and making as much as I could was foremost in my thoughts.

I busied myself writing book reviews, and because I had been, years before, a critic, albeit second string, was able to get a job reviewing an occasional Broadway show for the *Daily News*. My career as the Great American Novelist was on hold while I earned as much cash as I could to buy a decent suit and a new dress for Cherish for her gallery opening. I even entertained the hope that the paper would eventually hire me full-time as drama critic.

The spring openings were numerous, and I was able to review three or four shows a week. I decided to make hay while I could, knowing that, by summer, most of the theaters would close down because of the heat and not reopen until fall with the new season of shows.

During the summer, I thought, I will begin the actual writing of my new book.

I was getting tired of the struggle of daily life, tired of the condition of abject poverty that we had endured over the past few years in our determination to chase our artistic endeavors, Cherish and I. If her gallery show proved successful, as I prayed it would, and sometimes even *feared* it would, I could not bear to live off of Cherish's success, with her being seen as my meal ticket. I am ashamed to admit that I lived in dread of the day she would come to her senses and leave me. And during this period my fear of losing her became even more acute than ever.

Cherish enjoyed going to the theater with me. There was little time after the show for a late dinner, because I would have to go to the newspaper offices to compose and hand in a review for the morning run, so at around six o'clock we'd ride the El uptown and I would take her to a little Italian joint called Nino's on Forty-Third Street for spaghetti, or we'd have chicken fricassee at Schrafft's, with plenty of time to make the eight o'clock curtain. The last weeks before her gallery show, when she was too busy finishing canvases, I'd invite Anthony or Mark to see a play. On those evenings, Tony picked up the bill at Sardi's, and Mark preferred we dine on steak and drink at the 300 Club on Fifty-Fourth Street. I hadn't seen much of Daniel, except when our little club got together—the club we had begun to call among ourselves, The Murder Club.

Thanks to Anthony, we all left our egos at the door. Soon we became each other's sounding boards, and this helped tremendously in our personal instruction. Even Anthony admitted that he was becoming a better technician in the art of mystery writing.

Things changed one sultry night in late May 1929.

Unusual for that time of year, Manhattan was a furnace, a preview of the miserable heat of summer that was to come. When we all met at Marie's we took a table outside, under the vines, out on the back "porch," as Marie liked to call the little courtyard. Other than a hanging lantern pooling light over our table, the space was swallowed up in shadows cast by the mulberry tree at the courtyard's center. We were the only customers remaining outside when we finished our meals, or so we thought.

Trevor Hunter had brought a bottle of gin he had distilled in his "lab," which we all assumed was a euphemism for a still in his bathtub.

We decided to remain there for our talk rather than going to Anthony's after we'd eaten. The air was cooler under the vines, under the canopy of the mulberry tree with the slatted wooden bench circling its trunk.

We asked Marie for glasses and ice, and we five sat back and talked, not about our work, but about the business of writing: publishers, agents, lawyers, and all the compromises artists are expected to make.

I suppose it was the change in venue, which encouraged a more relaxed discussion, along with the gin, which softened our tongues, and the cooler air, which served as balm over our feverish brows after the stifling heat of the day, that prompted Cousins to tell us about the theft of his work by Mycroft Publishing.

This was not exactly news to any of us. But I was the only member of our group privy to the names of the culprits who had plagiarized Daniel's work; the others didn't know all of the details until Cousins laid out the story. They just figured his accusations were an excuse for the dry spell he was suffering. Hunter commented that although there were a number of unscrupulous people in the publishing world, it was unlikely to happen to Daniel again.

"Anyway, Daniel," he assured him, "we are all friends, here; you are safe with us. We are witnesses on your behalf, should anyone in future try to claim your efforts as their own." We all smiled and nodded encouragement.

It was Mark Wendt, upon hearing the names of publisher, Jim Morrow, and the accused-plagiarist author, Frederick Feldman, who dropped the bomb about the men's suspected sexual affair. These new revelations were bandied among us for a time like gossip at a ladies' garden party. Mark Wendt's new, lurid tidbit about the men's sexual peccadilloes appeared to release something in Cousins, although I couldn't, at the time, say just how or why he was set free of his demons. His spirits were raised, and I chalked it up to the idea that he now felt his claim of plagiarism justified, his accusation proven at last, as if the men's deviant sexual behavior, their depravity, attested to their crime against him.

And then Daniel Cousins said savagely, "I could kill those fucking queers."

"Daniel!" I protested with a nervous laugh. His vehemence had startled me, albeit justified from his point of view.

"Yes, I could kill them—if only I could get away with it!"

"If only," repeated Anthony. "*If only!* Those are words pregnant with possibility; words, too, heavy with regret. *If only....*"

"You should write a book, Daniel—a fiction book about this," said Wendt. "I mean fiction—the names are changed to protect the *blah-blah-blah.*"

"You can make it a murder mystery, Daniel," said Anthony Young, encouraging him. "Yes, you *must* write it as a murder mystery."

"Yes! Murder, of course," said Mark Wendt. "Write it in the first person."

"Who gets killed?" asked Daniel Cousins.

"Oh, you kill the publisher and the writer, of course. Very satisfying for you. Very cathartic. Revenge in absentia, so to speak," said Anthony.

"I'll bet there are a dozen possible twists on that one!" I said.

"Yes," agreed Anthony Young. "Take your pick, boy: Writer kills plagiarist author or plagiarist author kills the writer of the original work. Whoever does what to whomever winds up trying to prove his innocence—"

"Or," interrupted Hunter, "there is the blackmail scheme that leads to murder. Decide who blackmails whom, of course. You have forbidden sex and passion and money and fame and greed and revenge—"

"Not to mention suspense," said Anthony Young.

"But, now that you have a theme, it's only a springboard, Daniel," I said to encourage him.

Daniel Cousins smiled a grateful, pathetic little smile that barely turned up his lips.

"Yes," he said quietly, "it is a basis for a good story. I can see it. I think I could even do a good job of it. But, I might just go mad replaying in my head what these men did to me. And yet, if I killed them first, got my revenge, then I could write my story without going mad!"

"Yes, Daniel, and then after you've published your story, you do understand that the police will come and arrest you for murder?" said Anthony Young with a chuckle.

"Well," said Mark Wendt, "he'll sell more books if he's a notorious killer."

"And he'll have lots of women who will write to him and want to reform him," said Trevor.

"Sometimes I'm not sure what's more important to me," said Daniel, "a career as a successful author, or getting even with the bastards who screwed me over."

"Sure, you do!" A voice rang out from the dark regions of the courtyard, and I turned, thinking it was Marie's husband, the café's cook, calling out to us from the kitchen door.

It wasn't he, but a booming voice with a sure and cocky ring.

Stephen Shaw appeared from out of the shadows like an apparition and walked toward us from around the trunk of the mulberry tree. He stopped just short of total illumination from the hanging lantern. His hulking presence was disconcerting. The ghost of Hamlet's father came to mind with a frightening twist: This ghost was an errant soul clinging to the world of the living, albeit best assigned to a forsaken netherworld.

"You'll never be free until you know retribution," he said.

Cousins, whose back was to the tree, had turned sharply at the sound of Shaw's voice. From the backlighting I saw the hair rise up on the back of his neck. Anthony Young's flaccid jowls quivered in double-take.

Shaw stepped into the pool of light. "Whose cock do I have to suck to get a drink around here?"

"Nobody's I want to know, Shaw," Hunter chortled. "How long have you been playing with yourself out there in the dark, you damned pervert?"

"Long enough to know this man's got a hard-on he's got to tend to before he can set down to work." He patted Daniel's shoulder, and I watched him cringe under Shaw's touch.

Stephen Shaw grabbed a chair from a vacant table and in one sweep brought it to rest between Cousins and Young. Hunter filled his own glass with gin and pushed it across the table toward Shaw, who knocked it back in one fast swig. He exhaled with a loud grunt and smacked his lips, and then considered the empty glass as if assessing the quality of the liquor before passing it back to Hunter for another round.

Again, he knocked back the booze, and then said: "Thing is, how do you kill a man and not get caught?"

I knew he was serious in spite of the mocking cackle he emitted before downing the dregs of the glass.

Breaking the heavy silence that had fallen like a shroud over the table, Hunter said, "That's the rub."

"Yeah, well, if you've not the balls to make them pay with their lives, why not first make them pay from their pockets?"

"Blackmail?" I spurted out, unaware I'd spoken my thoughts aloud.

"Sure, *sure!* He's got the dirt on them queers, now, don't you, Daniel?"

"Forget it, Stephen," said Hunter. "Things rarely fare well for the blackmailer. We're talking about writing books."

"Yeah, it's true. You have to have heart—and balls—to run a scheme like that, and our Daniel here, hasn't got the heart—or the balls—for such a venture. Killing is better. But how to?"

"Have you ever killed a man, Shaw?" I asked, and almost immediately regretted the question.

What compelled me to speak? I didn't really want to hear his confession and know of his deeds; I wanted no part of Stephen Shaw and I knew that any association with him would only lead to trouble. I wanted to bolt out of the courtyard. What had been a most pleasant evening had suddenly turned menacing with his arrival. But, I kept my seat as if tied to it by invisible, inescapable bonds. Shaw looked me over, all the while wearing a cunning leer that passed for a smile.

He nodded, ambiguously, and I knew he was not about to reveal any of his secrets. Then he turned his attention on Anthony Young, and I could see the history professor back away slightly from Shaw's foul breath. I realized then how terrified Anthony was of this man, and that try as he might to hold his ground under the scrutiny of Shaw's eyes, Anthony's fear did not abate. I heard the unconscious and sharp intake of air and a nearly inaudible little whinnying that escaped his lips.

Shaw heard it, too, for he laughed, and turning his attention on his empty glass said with riducule, "Tony, Tony, Tony . . ."

"What's that all *about*?" spat out Young, spittle flying across the glaring light from the lantern, a rash instantly appearing over his collar, moving up like a tide along his jowls to his cheeks. He shifted in his seat and indignantly stated, "What in God's name do you want, man!"

"Well, now, Tony, there's no need to get all hot under the collar. You, more than anyone here, can relate to the, *uh*, the *raping* Danny took—"

"Shut the hell up, you cretin!"

"But what have you ever done about it, I ask you?"

"*I order you to stop!*" yelled Young, bolting from his chair and sending it crashing into the table behind ours.

"Really, Shaw," said Hunter, "you're such a bully sometimes."

"I will not remain here as long as this—*this*—"

"Sit down, Tony," said Hunter with great authority. "Stephen, if you want to stay, show some respect."

"I have nothing *but* respect for Tony, here. He, more than anyone at this table, has known a great success through his mystery novels, if that's the kind of book one wants to write, of course: a middling entertainment for the middling mind."

"That's a backhanded compliment, if ever I heard one," said Mark Wendt. "Odd, don't you think, that we're all gathered here tonight to learn exactly *how* to create what you call middling entertainment!"

Daniel Cousins snickered and said, "At least Tony doesn't get sued and brought to court for defamation like some muckrakers I can think of."

"All right, boys," chuckled Shaw, nodding and acknowledging the truth of Daniel's accusation. "I can see how you might want to defend the professor here. He's not a bad sort, that I know. And he's stood up to me, so I have to credit him that, I suppose." He struck a match on his boot and lit a cigarette, amusement still on his face.

And then he stuck out his hand toward Anthony Young, as a gesture of peace. Anthony looked at it: the hairy wrist, the bulbous sinews, the knotty knuckles, the blunted fingertips. A more attractive claw was a hawk's talon. But, then, of course, in spite of the side-handed offer of peace, Shaw *was* a hawk, and Young had always been his intended prey.

Anthony turned away with a look of disgust, retrieved his chair, and resumed his place at the table. I offered him a cigarette, which he took, and

I lit it for him, steadying his trembling hand as I held the match.

Shaw's appearance had put a damper on the evening, but not to give him the advantage of having driven us off, we remained a few minutes longer talking about nothing of any consequence.

And then he said, "You boys," looking at me and then Daniel and then Mark, "you boys, you throw around ideas for plotting to kill—for your stories. You'll just wind up with the silliness of puzzles; pointless puzzles to piece together, without any real guts to the stories, like that Christie woman writes, like what Tony, here, has been passing over to thrill dimwitted women over the years. You all think you can get into the mind of a killer so easily? You think you can write your make-believe books and there'll be truth behind them? There can't be truth unless you know what it's like, unless you, yourself, have ever committed murder. Ever kill someone? Can you really say that you know what it *feels* like to kill?"

What it feels like to kill.

My skin crawled. I tried to shake off my feeling of dread, but it wasn't easy. He continued: "You can't write about love, unless you've known love. You can't write about what it feels like to crush a man's skull unless you've crushed one yourself and smelled the blood, and heard the crack of bone, and watched the life drain from his eyes . . ."

"That's absurd," said Trevor.

"Puzzles, that's all you'll get. Bloodless puzzles like your friend Conan Doyle pens. No guts, no heart, no . . . nothing of substance."

But Shaw's presence and his cruel goading of Anthony Young served to change the tone of our talks for the better, from one of professional detachment to a darker, more visceral mood. What had before been the simple exchanging of ideas for our murder mystery plots—the mere objectivity of the *how* and *when* and *where* the ax murderer would execute his mad plan on his victims—now became discussions on how to wreak revenge on our individual demons. At first, I figured this strange evolution that had swept over our talks was simply expressions of our own particular frustrations: Mark's sudden and unendurable loss after the death of his grand passion; the theft of Daniel's work and his subsequent paranoia. Empathetically, I couldn't help but be pulled into their worlds and the shame of their suffered injustices. These personal introspections, I thought, though not always pleasant, gave us new insight into our characters' minds. Still, I kept my shameful family secret to myself.

Shaw invariably would show up late in the evening, but from now on he behaved quite civilly toward Anthony Young. There was no more baiting or insinuations toward any of us. In spite of the smirk that always rested on his face, it was a complete reversal, and I chalked up Stephen Shaw's past offenses as having been caused by drunkenness and his opium habit.

Anthony Young weathered Shaw's abrasive edge, avoiding eye contact with the man, and Shaw mostly listened rather than engaged in our talks. The dynamics of their behavior toward one another gave me pause. They couldn't stand each other, and yet, once a week, they did.

Why did Anthony tolerate his presence? Why was Shaw even bothering with us? He had made it perfectly clear that he thought our "mystery puzzles" foolish. Was it for his own amusement, or was there something that Shaw knew about him that Anthony feared might be revealed if he remained hostile toward him?

I couldn't help thinking about the confrontation that first night in the courtyard when Shaw busted in with the comment likening Cousins' predicament with Young's. He had referred to the plagiarism of Daniel's book as a "rape," and he had implied some sort of plagiarism involving Young. Odd choice of words at the time. Had he meant that Anthony had been dealt the same injustice, or that Anthony had stolen someone else's work? While at Princeton, perhaps? Was that the reason why Anthony behaved sheepishly in Shaw's presence? In the meantime, I watched as Shaw became more solicitous toward Young, which further raised my suspicions, sending my imagination off to extremes of invention involving blackmail and extortion.

During the first three weeks of July, we didn't meet. Anthony had commitments for lectures out of town, with a stop at Newport, he said, to visit his cousins at their summer residence there. Mark was the guest of the theater critic, Alexander Woollcott, at his retreat on Neshobi Island in Lake Bomoseen, where he would be expected to play croquet with other illustrious stage stars, several of whom were old friends from his days as a Broadway hoofer. Daniel had been summoned by his mother to spend his vacation time at her estate in Glen Cove. There was to be a celebration for her sixtieth birthday. While there he took a fancy to a young woman from New Jersey, a cousin three times removed, and whom he had not met since she was seven years old. He took an extra week off from his job at the *Saturday Evening Post,* which got him fired from his position as copywriter. I heard through Marie that Trevor had gone to Washington D.C. on business.

It was during this hiatus that a series of events occurred that upset my world.

I was informed by letter from the editor of the *Daily News* that I would no longer be employed by their newspaper as drama critic. No reason given, just a termination. Just as I was beginning to earn some decent money.

I was shaken and angry, and I wanted to know why I was let go. Had I insulted the Shuberts, who continued to produce rubbish? Was it to do with some disgruntled star who was a friend of the publisher?

I stormed down to the offices on Park Place to demand an explanation. But by the time I arrived and crossed through the chaos that was the newsroom and trudged along the last part of my journey to the office of the executive editor, my anger had turned to fear and I was determined to beg for my job back.

Frank McCarthy, a no-nonsense straight-shooter, laid it out bluntly. The boss found out I was the author of pornographic books. A "morals clause" or something to that effect; my ears were ringing.

When I asked why he believed such a thing, he replied, "Cut the crap, Stringer, Harvey Price plays cards with Patterson. He's the source."

"But, *nobody* knows—"

"Give me a break. *Everybody* knows, now that Price told the boss."

I started to back out of the office door. The clicking of typewriter keys echoed through the big room like a mocking chorus of cicadas.

"Stringer, for what it's worth, nobody gives a crap about the porn. Patterson's probably read the books himself. Thing is, now he knows it was you. *You*, the guy who panned his wife's sister in that crappy show that closed anyway."

"*What* show?"

"I don't know! Something about dancing nurses."

I tried to think, to remember a show with dancing nurses, a production that was *so memorable* that I could forget it so soon—as if remembering was important, would get me my job back.

"Goodbye and good luck, Stringer," said Frank McCarthy as he rushed out the door past me, a sheaf of papers clutched in his hand, screaming out, "Copy boy, copy boy!" and making a beeline for a reporter across the newsroom.

I wasn't sure what hit me hardest: being out of work, my reputation being tarnished, or having my identity compromised by Harvey Price.

The drunken son-of-a-bitch! All of them, all of those hypocrite sons-of-bitches! Morals clause—I didn't even have a contract with the paper. I realized that it was only a matter of time before the magazine people would find out, and then I wouldn't even have the book reviews, either. *Goddamn Price!*

Why, *why* did I write that stuff? I asked myself. I knew the answer, but I couldn't help the self-recrimination. *I was fucking hungry! Cherish was hungry! Hungry, for God's sake. Living on toast and boiled rice and beans. Why else write that crap? Goddamn Price!*

The rent had been past due by two months when I landed the job at the *Daily News.* I had hoped to find a dentist soon. I needed a tooth pulled, it was a constant ache, and now it would all be on *her* shoulders. Cherish's.

Her artwork had been critically well received at the gallery, but she hadn't made many sales of her canvases. I didn't want her modeling for other artists. I had tried to overcome the feelings I had about her standing nude before those men. My imagination tortured me. When I looked at Cherish I felt conflicted: I wanted to trust in her faithfulness and dedication, but I found it difficult to contend with my feelings of jealousy.

Could we survive another winter in our cold flat? Would she finally see me for the loser I was and run off with the successful Carlos Miguel Hernandez? That fine example of masculine prowess?

I wished then, as I once again found myself fallen to the bottom of the heap of aspiring success stories, that I had the money to get drunk or the courage to kill myself. Because how could I ever get back up again? My reputation was shot. I would have to write under a *nom de plume*, if I could ever get a reputable publisher again.

I walked through the streets, oblivious of the traffic, of the noontide of passersby from the office buildings around Wall Street. The summer sun was unrelenting and I soon began to feel lightheaded. My mouth was dry and my shirt soaked with sweat. I passed a pushcart vendor near Trinity Church. Digging for change, I found enough to buy a Coke, which I guzzled as the traffic of cars and pedestrians flowed past me. I was a log stuck in the stream of progress.

I walked into the churchyard for relief from the sun, its tall trees shading the ancient gravestones, and settled on a bench.

I looked around me. I was in the silent company of the men and women who had forged a nation. Revolutionary War Generals, their wives and daughters, infants and sons; Alexander Hamilton, Robert Fulton, and John Jacob Astor lie here, alongside scores of long-forgotten colonial dignitaries, Continental Congressmen, ships' captains, commodores, and sail-makers. Why should I hope that my pathetic efforts as a writer would matter at all in the great scheme of things? What could I ever hope to accomplish that would justify my efforts? And why was it so important that I do something important? Why did I need to . . . *matter*? We all became dust, eventually.

Sparrows in the bush twittered at my foolishness.

The morning *Times* rested on the bench, old news left behind, and I reached for it, my fingers claiming it like a spurious gift. A sense of dread and failure swept over me as I tucked it under my elbow.

I don't know for how long I sat there, but the next thing I remember I was getting on the Sixth Avenue El at Rector Street. Screeching brakes woke me from my reverie of doom, so I got off and walked the Village streets toward home, clutching the paper, skirting a kid rolling an iron tire ring, a gang shooting marbles, young mothers in cotton print dresses pushing prams, a couple of old Sicilian shawlies arguing with gestures and shouts in indecipherable babble. I was stopped in my tracks at the *he-haw* blast of a car horn, narrowly escaping being run down as I crossed the traffic-packed street. The march of progress kept on while I struggled to keep up.

The streets were teeming with kids and bicycles and venders hawking their goods, and the rumble of the Sixth Avenue El behind me gave over to the approaching thunder of the Ninth Avenue El, brakes screaming hysterically. A barrage of human exchanges—the shouts of street workers, of babies screaming and mothers scolding, all trivial dramas compared to the urgent voice of NBC announcer Graham MacNamee calling the Giants–Indians game—pouring out from open tenement windows.

The kitchens of Italian women sent the fragrant aroma of tomato sauce simmering through the air. The warm, yeasty smell of bread and sugary cakes wafted dreamily from a bakery on Hudson Street and made me almost swoon with hunger before I was assaulted by the wretched stench of rotting garbage overflowing the steel cans, abuzz with flies, lined up at the curbs in front of tenements like beaten prisoners before a firing squad.

I'd not eaten since the previous evening and the soda that had quelled my immediate thirst had only made me crave more. I dodged traffic, urged on in my pressing thirst, forgetting for a few minutes my tumble from grace.

My head was splitting from the onslaught of noise and heat. I reached for my nose-drops to ease my burning sinuses.

Finally, I turned into the doorway next to the shoemaker's shop. The sweet smell of leather and polish was redolent in the air as I climbed to the second-floor flat. The hum of revolving wheel belts faded at the landing as an aria from *La Bohème* drifted out from the Victrola in the apartment of Mr. Vitelli, the retired and poverty-stricken tenor from the chorus of the Met. Another pathetic failure.

Fumbling for my key, I saw that the door was slightly ajar. In my rush to confront my editor I had never bothered to close, let alone lock it.

What would anyone bother to steal? A few second-hand books? A couple of Cherish's paintings on the walls that no one wanted to buy? Tattered armchairs? Beat-up pots and pans? The only thing of value to me was my Royal typewriter and the counterpane over our bed, painted by Cherish and depicting a moonlit scene of the New York skyline in rich tones of blue.

How was I going to break the news to her about . . . everything? Would she lose patience?

I asked her once, after the first bloom of my first success had faded and I was in a despondent and stagnant state of being, "Why on earth do you love me?"

"Why, silly?" she replied, looking at me with amusement in her eyes.

"Yes, why? What is it about me that I should be deserving of your love?"

When she saw I was serious and the question wasn't arbitrary, she looked me over the way she usually looks at one of her finished paintings to assess its worth. After a few seconds a little frown quivered on her brow, and she said, "I don't know. I just do."

I suppose I didn't look satisfied with her answer, that I expected more, wanting some reason that I had to strive to live up to. She picked up on my disappointment.

"What? Do you want me to tell you that I love you because you are handsome? You're no Valentino. Do you want me to say that I love you because you are kind? You aren't always kind. That you are encouraging and that you believe in me, my talent? Lots of people say those things to me, but I don't love them. Is it because you are brilliant? Everybody knows you are, so that puts me in with the crowd of mere admirers. Should I say I love you because you need me? Because I *need* you? I can't and I won't qualify my love so mundanely."

"So, you won't answer the question."

"No," she said, turning that serious and direct gaze on me.

"Or, is it that you *can't* answer the question?"

"If I try too hard to figure out *why*, I might find out that I fell in love with you capriciously, and I would then have to take stock and eventually come to the conclusion that it was all one big mistake."

She smiled a wily little smile, and said, "Idiot. What do you want me to do, recite Elizabeth Barrett Browning, for God's sake?"

I wanted to find her now, to hold her, to have her reassure me that my life wasn't over, but my sense of failure was too great to risk delivering to her yet another disappointment. She might finally ask herself the question I had once asked her. *Why?* Why do I love this man? And she might come to see that our relationship had been a drastic mistake. And then I thought, *was I so insecure of her love for me?*

She was no doubt upstairs in her attic studio at work on a new canvas. She never stopped trying. She just kept on creating. Why shouldn't I forget these fears and just carry on, too?

I glanced at my typewriter, the ramrod sentinel dominating my desk, standing as patiently and stoically as any butler awaiting his master's call to duty. I knew what I had to do. I grabbed a pencil and sat down in the armchair with the newspaper. The butler would have to wait.

I circled two waiters' jobs, one for an office clerk, and an ad from a bakery looking for a delivery truck driver. The last seemed most promising. It meant possibly free day-old bread and was close by. I could walk to work and save the subway or streetcar fare. But if I could get a waiter's job as well, working nights, I wouldn't mind, and Cherish might never have to deal with my unemployment.

Goddamn Harvey Price!

The ads required that I apply in person. I would pull myself together, wash and shave and put on a clean shirt, I decided, ripping out the page, folding it and sliding it into my jacket pocket. I was folding up the rest of the newspaper when I saw the headline of a story on page two:

Author Found Dead!
Suicide by Hanging

The body of writer Frederick Feldman was discovered last night in his West End Avenue apartment. The author of Hold Back the Night, *a much acclaimed first novel, published in 1924 by James Morrow & Company, was discovered after friends called the police after Mr. Feldman failed to attend a dinner party in his honor in celebration of his thirty-fifth birthday.*

There followed a short bio of the dead man with quotes of acclaim from a couple of well-known critics about his book. *Daniel's book*—if what Daniel kept saying was true and not the ravings of a paranoid mind.

My first thought was to call Daniel to tell him, or ask if he already knew about the suicide. But, I had more pressing matters to attend to, the afternoon was progressing, and I was determined to find a job by the end of the day.

I was able to secure two jobs that afternoon: the bakery deliveryman's job—just three blocks from the apartment—and, after rushing uptown to the Melville Club, a waiter's job. Changed into my one good suit, unearthed from the back of the coat closet, complete with shirtfront, too, which I had bought for ten bucks from a second-hand shop on Canal Street to wear for Cherish's gallery show opening, and wearing the old black patent leathers, now stiff from age and disuse but looking like new with the wipe of a dust cloth, I was quite presentable, if one didn't notice my socks. I hoped that I would never be asked to sit down during the interview. Anyway, I got the job as beverage waiter in the club's Clipper Lounge, three nights a week.

Unbelievably, I felt as high and as joyful as if I'd won a Pulitzer for the relief I felt. I would arrive at four-thirty each morning to load up the bread truck to start deliveries at five, Monday through Friday. At ten, another round of deliveries and done by one o'clock. On Tuesdays, Thursdays, and Fridays, I would arrive at the Midtown men's club, and begin my shift at four o'clock and end at midnight, or thereabouts. I still had weekends to write and a couple weekday afternoons and evenings, too. Over the next couple of weeks it was all about learning delivery routes, and then, changing into the uniform provided by the club (the cost of which was seven dollars, to be taken out of my pay over the next month), I waited on the club's membership. I threw myself into this work with great earnestness, determined to earn a decent living, even if it meant that for the rest of the summer I was absent from our regular writers' talks.

Chapter Three

By chance, I met Anthony one autumn morning as he was walking along Washington Avenue. I was stepping up into the driver's seat of my delivery truck when he stopped, caught my eye, and called out to me. It was then that I was bound to explain my circumstances.

Thanks to his innate grace, Anthony smiled and said he was glad I'd found employment, and he didn't ask why I hadn't been kept on at the newspaper. This kindness led me to confide the truth about my dismissal. He shook his head in disbelief and then laughed and threw off the very idea that I should have lost the job because of my penning the books.

"Dear boy," he began with avuncular bravado, patting my shoulder. "These people are small-minded imbeciles! You were a very good critic, and it is their loss, the fools! Now, put that nonsense right behind you. It's a temporary setback. Deliver your bread. We've missed you these past weeks. The boys and I thought you had given up on us and on writing—or that you were actually too busy writing your new book. Alas, sometimes it is necessary to put things aside in order to—to see to everyday demands. But can't you join us on Tuesday evenings? We've lots to discuss!"

I saw a marked changed in Anthony Young's demeanor. It was difficult to put a finger on it, but he appeared more in command of himself, more assured of his place of importance in our Murder Club. He was, after all, at the heart of our group, and he had been more than generous with his help as we began to weave our individual tales of mystery. But, as we parted ways I noted that in spite of the impeccable tailoring, the tidy professor, who never took a step out of his row-house without a flower in his lapel, a pin in his tie, and a blinding shine on his shoes, appeared to have acquired a youthful spring to his step.

Seeing Tony made me yearn to get to work on a new book. I arranged to be free of my duties at the club on Tuesday nights, agreeing to work Wednesdays instead, exchanging nights with a fellow attending evening classes at City University.

The next week, on a muggy October night, I walked into the courtyard of Romany Marie's and was greeted by Mark, Daniel, Trevor, and Anthony with a welcome usually reserved for soldiers returning from war.

The change in Anthony was not merely an impression I had had when he stopped me on the street; it was clearly evident tonight. Aside from the fact that he had lost weight—he no longer carried that pouch along his waistline—his entire demeanor radiated an easy casualness, replacing his usual formal carriage. In the spirit of appreciation, I suggested that a young woman must have entered his life, and was sorry to have embarrassed the man, for he blushed, as was his cross to bear in life, and it was Trevor Hunter who spoke and explained that "the new book Tony had put to bed was considered by his new publisher to be "a notable work of brilliance. He's just been basking too long in the radiance."

"You do go too far, Trevor!"

"Why, I am beside myself with envy, Tony," extolled Hunter. "It is the work of a genius, I suppose, although you haven't let me see it."

The maiden-aunt persona that was so much a part of one's initial impression of Anthony Young might have been abandoned, but for a brief moment peeked through when he twitched his mouth with false modesty at the praise and replied that if he had done anything at all that was good, it was because of the assistance of Trevor Hunter, who had given him all the forensic and scientific data he had needed for crafting his book, "and," he added, with a gracious sweep of his hand, "the support of my fellow club members."

"But, you never discussed—we don't even know what the book is about, Tony. I don't think that's fair," said Daniel Cousins, expressing a rather confident tone, one devoid of—should I say, *resentment*? It was an immediate impression, this newly adopted tone, because Daniel's usual comments had always seemed tinged with a whine of displeasure, of *envy*. I chalked it up to feelings of safe harbor within our little congregation.

"You haven't mentioned it at all!" said Daniel, laughing.

Interesting development, I thought, while I had been absent these past months.

Mark said to Anthony, "That's right. You never shared anything about it."

"Ah, yes, but you all inspired me to write it. You see, I have become fearless thanks to you all, and I have left the series that was so popular, so lucrative, to approach in this new book a more visceral study of vengeance."

"Well, all right, its theme is vengeance. But what's the story about?" I asked, glad that the focus was on Tony and not on me, having to explain my prolonged absence from our meetings.

"Yes," said Mark with an impatient tone. "Enough with the accolades about the book. What the hell is it about?" Mark flashed a wicked little smile. He really seemed to have recovered from the tragedy of his loss of last winter, and one couldn't deny he was one of those men who, having borne and then risen from his troubles, was made more attractive for having survived. His face had narrowed, the boyish features honed and chiseled by grief and maturity. He was no longer the chorus boy, the Broadway hoofer of a decade past. He seemed more solid, more substantial, and his experience and suffering actually made him handsomer—more alive, more vibrant. I envied him for it. I was the sort who was just getting more and more haggard through my years of struggle.

"What is it about . . . what *is it about?*" prefaced Anthony, obviously enjoying the suspense he was building among his colleagues. A sly smile passed over his full, red lips. "All right, it's about a man who waits nearly twenty years to have his revenge on the men who caused his humiliation, and how the crime he commits serves to heal his crippling wounds and sets his spirit free."

"Redemption through revenge?" I asked.

"Revenge is a dish best served cold?" asked Daniel Cousins.

"None of those clichés, boy, though it carries much truth, I admit. It makes for the perfect murder," nodded Young. "And do you know why?"

"I suppose," said Mark Wendt, "that a crime committed in the heat of the moment is likely to get one caught. But twenty years after the injury, well . . ."

"Yes, that is so," agreed Young. "As Daniel said, a dish best served cold.

"It is the distance in time and place that can make all the difference, especially if you, the killer, have had no contact with your victim, no dealings whatsoever over the years, so that you are never even remotely considered a suspect in the murder investigation. But, most importantly, if your victim's transgression against you all those years ago was an act so heinous, so despicable that he wishes to forget what he had done, to bury it, and has never dared to share what he did with another living soul, well, then, who would ever suspect a ghost from the distant past responsible for murder? There would be no motive against you—the killer. And why? *Because your victim was never culpable for having committed a crime for which you sought revenge!*"

"It does sound like a plan for perfect murder," said Daniel Cousins, and I could see the wheels turning in his head.

Again, I was struck by Daniel's full engagement. A lot had changed during my absence. Daniel appeared to have found some degree of solace—if that's the right word to describe the apparent lift in his spirits—in the suicide death of the man who stole his book. In his heart of hearts, he must have felt vindicated, and because he did, the resentment he carried of his failure was somewhat dispelled. I felt this was very sad.

Although I'd had every intention of doing so, I had never telephoned nor had a chance to discuss with Daniel the news headline I had seen the very day that I was fired from the paper. In fact, this night was the first I'd seen of Daniel, since taking on the two jobs.

When I walked into the café earlier, I had a minute to speak with Daniel before the others arrived. He said had been hard at work on his new book. I was about to mention Feldman's suicide when he began telling me that our weekly meetings were his only time away from his typewriter. When the others arrived, the mood was not right to ask about such things. Still, Daniel had the look of a driven man, no longer the depressed and hopeless fellow of a year ago, but one determined to succeed.

Whether it was the result of the news of Frederick Feldman's suicide that brought Daniel's improved condition, or the excitement of finally being able to craft his first book after a long dry spell, I didn't know, but I was glad for him. Truth be told, I also felt left behind from the others, late for the party, and suddenly I felt rising in my gut the urgent need to catch up with a new creation of my own.

My observations about my fellow Murder Club members and their amazing metamorphoses were dashed when a familiar, if unwelcome, voice boomed out: "Congratulations, Tony."

It was Shaw, appearing late as was his habit. Ridiculously, I felt that his tardiness was deliberate, that he was always lurking somewhere nearby, waiting for the moment to arrive in the conversation when he could best disrupt the discussion.

"It sounds like you finally put your story down on paper," he said, and a pall fell over the group.

As everyone remained mute, it provided Shaw with an opening. "You lived the tale, Tony."

And so, Stephen Shaw had reverted to his old ways tonight. But why?

Anthony Young gathered his wits and with resigned acceptance said in a quiet, even voice, "Yes. It came to me easily—the plot."

Trevor Hunter nodded and calmly stated, "Ingenious!" But the telltale twitch in his left cheek betrayed his alarm.

"If that's how you want to tell it," said Shaw. "I thought it was a personal story."

"There are elements of a true tale about it, that is so . . ." said Tony, nodding, his eyes rigidly fixed on the table as he tapped a forefinger on his drinking glass. His jowls reddened. "An incident at school I heard about when I was a college boy."

"It's always best to write about what you know," agreed Shaw.

"As a springboard, perhaps. Sometimes a story or a phrase can get one started. Yes." Tony stood up from his chair, fetched his Borselino and gloves and his walking stick, glanced at his pocket watch, and gave excuses that he had to see off a friend crossing to France tonight, bidding us to stay, and that he would see us next Tuesday for a celebratory dinner at Delmonico's.

As he fled the garden, Shaw leaned over us, nodded, and flashed us his crooked-toothed grin before beating a path after Anthony.

"What the hell . . .?" said Mark.

"Have you read the book, Trevor?" I asked.

The twitch again, and a fleeting frown knitted his heavy brows. But his features quickly relaxed into an expression of indifference as he looked me in the eye and said, "You know how much Shaw rattles Tony."

"But Anthony said his novel won't be out until next spring. How does Shaw know anything about it?"

"Who knows?" snapped Trevor, uncharacteristically, his speech more starkly British than ever.

"But you know something about the story, don't you?" Mark said. "Tony just said that you helped him with it."

"With current toxicology, the latest forensics, that sort of thing. I never read the manuscript, if that's what you're getting at. I don't know anything more than you do."

"He said it was a story he heard when he was a university student," I said.

"Well," stated Trevor officiously, violently turning those lash-less, black-hooded gray eyes on me, "we'll just have to wait for the book to be published to find out, won't we?"

As if Trevor had willed it to put an end to my questions, it started to rain, a downpour, sending us into the cover of the café.

A bedraggled young woman was reciting poetry, composed, no doubt, from her own nightmares. Very dark and gloomy, very bad stuff. As there were no tables available that we might continue our discussion, we four stood silently in the café's front door, formulating our own thoughts—at least I was—and waiting for the rain to subside. Trevor looked a statue: grim, unmoving, and staring vacantly at the sad girl reciting her trash, not a syllable penetrating his stony exterior. Suddenly, he turned and pushed through the door, out into the rain, his fedora pulled low and his coat collar raised to meet the brim. Mark and I looked at each other, and there was the mention of a drink at Chumley's. I begged off. I was tired from my pre-dawn schedule, and after a few moments, I left the café to walk home through the rain.

I was just approaching the intersection of Barrow and Hudson Streets when the rain began to pour down with a newfound fury. The streets became rivers, gutter pipes rattled, street signs *rat-tat-tatted*, and the water hurling into the sewer drains swirled like whirlpools.

Automobiles sliced through torrents, dashing water along the sidewalks. Caught unaware, people scattered for cover; the younger and more carefree laughed joyfully at nature's spontaneity. People holed up in doorways and under precariously waterlogged awnings.

And then, it was as if God turned off the bath water, it stopped so suddenly.

I looked up from out my coat collar at the shimmering black field of wet pavement. The wind, which a moment ago had swept over the turbulent pools, died away. The city had been washed clean, and its distinctive smell, a mixture of car fumes and coal smoke, was gone, and the moist air was now redolent with the scent of water-soaked tree bark and autumn leaves. A fine mist haloed the streetlamps as a rolling fog crept slowly from the North River. I stepped off the curb and landed in a puddle so deep that I became drenched to the ankle of one foot, and before I could stop myself, l doubled the insult. I cursed the world.

As I sloshed into the street—distracted from watching for oncoming traffic by my dismay at the ruination of my only good pair of shoes—I was caught in the glaring headlights warning me of a danger far greater than soggy shoe-leather.

The taxi came to an abrupt halt, missing me by mere inches while sending a shower to complete my drenching. The cabbie squawked his horn, for effect or from frustration or downright meanness, but mostly to curse the fool at his fender.

Irate, I stepped back up to escape onto the curb but my heel missed its mark. I slipped on the slick metal sewer grate, fell back, and was stabbed first by a fire hydrant, and upon completing my fall, by the sharp edge of the curb. The pain was excruciating; I couldn't even suck in enough breath to gasp. My arm had struck, too, and I feared it was broken because the pain was so keen. Finally, I responded to the repetitious horn-honking, half rising from my cold bath, the trouser cuffs of my good tweeds weighted and dragging, one caught under my heel. The taxi barreled north on Hudson Street without a care. I cursed the world, the reckless cabbie, and the stabbing pain in my side.

A hand reached out from the dark to help me complete my rise, and a familiar voice asked if I was all right.

Trevor Hunter hulked over me, his gray eyes shadowed now from the brim of his hat. He took hold of my elbow and then led me toward a waiting taxi.

"Come this way," he said. And then, once in the taxi, he told the driver to continue on.

I was about to say, I live just a few blocks away, when the cab turned east, crossed Seventh Avenue and then Sixth, before continuing across Ninth Street.

"Here we are," said Trevor, as the taxi pulled up alongside a townhouse. Trevor exited the cab, handing the driver a couple of dollars. I began to say that I lived in the opposite direction, but Trevor must have read my mind, for he nodded and waved me on, saying, "Let's get you out of those wet clothes and into a dry martini."

"You've stolen that line," I chuckled painfully, my anger abating.

"Yes, but if you have to steal, steal from the best. By God," he drawled as he led the way up the steps toward the entrance of the lovely townhouse, "I've been waiting eons for just the right time to use that line!"

"So you should be thanking me for the opportunity?"

"Yes, thank you, Ernest," laughed Trevor.

He unlocked the door and I followed him into a dark foyer just as another round of rain began. Through another set of doors we entered into the main hall. He threw the light switch, and a chandelier hanging from an elaborate plaster medallion brightened the walnut paneling, and I was greeted with the warm jewel tones of Persian runners leading up the long stairs, acanthus-leaf wallpaper reaching to the ceiling moldings, and impressive panel doors leading into the main salon to our right.

"Drop those shoes and hang the coat and hat there," said Trevor, indicating the tall, beveled-mirrored bench. Wait here, Neptune's folly," he said, as he progressed into the salon. I did as instructed. A few moments later, Trevor tossed me a towel, and told me to follow him up the stairs. I did as I was told, and when we'd arrived on the landing, he entered the bathroom, turned on the water to the tub, and as the steam began to rise, I watched as he threw a handful of salts into the water.

"Epsom salts. Take a hot bath while I find you some dry clothes," he said. "That room on your left. I'll set some things out in there." He closed the door behind him.

I have to admit I felt awkward, uneasy at this hospitality, but I was shivering and my ribs hurt from the crash to the curb. The bathroom was lavish by my shabby standards, and within a few minutes I was stretched out in the deep claw-foot tub, the heat restoring my spirits. I could have stayed there for hours in the warmth, luxuriating in the comfort of the silky waters, the steam permeating my weary and shocked bones. There was a knock on the door, and Trevor peeked in to say he'd be down in the drawing room.

A half-hour later, I walked down the stairs in slightly baggy flannel trousers and a crisp white shirt under a cashmere blue cardigan. Remarkably, I was heeled in a pair of perfectly fitting Oxford brogues over Argyle hose. The man had provided everything, even the briefs.

"You'd make a fitting British country squire, Ernest," said Trevor, handing me a snifter of cognac and pointing me toward the wingchair beside the fire.

"Thank you for this," I said, leaning back in the chair, and Trevor must have seen me grimace, because he asked if I was badly hurt.

"Probably just bruised ribs," I replied. "Nothing that this won't cure," I said, taking a sip of the excellent cognac.

Trevor was stuffing his briar pipe with sweet-smelling tobacco, and while he continued through the ritual lighting and puffing, we sat silently for a few minutes. I looked around the well-appointed room, noting the dozens of photographs, daguerreotypes from the last century of stern ladies in neck-choking collars and gentlemen sporting mutton-chop whiskers.

On the grand piano that dominated the bay windows was a photograph of a younger, lankier Trevor, standing beside an older man.

"Your father, Trevor? In that photograph on the piano?

"Actually, that's me with my godfather, Arthur. Arthur Conan Doyle. Matter of fact, you are wearing his trousers and shoes."

"You're kidding," I laughed.

"Not at all. He left a suitcase at his hotel a few years ago, and after I retrieved it, he wired me not to bother to ship it over. It's been sitting in the back of my closet all these years. At least the clothes are being put to good use."

"I'll get these back to you, cleaned and—"

"Oh, don't bother. I doubt I'll chance upon another unfortunate chap soaked to the gills."

"I have to admit, the shoes fit perfectly," I said, admiring them. "If I didn't know better, I'd think you hadn't just chanced upon me at all."

"Then, you should rethink that."

"I don't—"

"Your first thought was correct. I followed you."

Suddenly, I had an uneasy feeling.

"Oh, don't look so worried," he chuckled, sitting down in the chair across from me. "I just wanted to talk with you, but before I could call your attention, you decided to take a swim. Had you not made a spectacle of yourself, I'd have suggested a drink at a speak, without risking my houseman's wrath at the sight of what this cat dragged in. Fortunately—for both of us—it's his evening off. But, he did leave me a lovely casserole, which I popped into the oven while you were bathing. It smells like it is almost ready. You must be starving! And then we can talk. We'll eat in here," he said, and then proceeded to bring over a large tea-table from the corner, which he set down between our wingchairs.

He reached into his jacket pocket and removed a freshly laundered handkerchief, handed it to me, and said, "Before you leave, I must remember to fix you a remedy for those sinuses of yours. Those drops aren't doing the trick." With that, he left the room.

He is a queer one, I thought when he left to fetch the supper. I couldn't quite figure him out.

I had never known him to be as solicitous as now, treating me to the comforts of his home.

As he was always polite and forthcoming in the company of the other men in our club, my initial impression that he was an intellectual snob had been quickly put to rest. And yet, I had not been completely wrong, because there was this air of detachment about him. He was guarded, if not aloof. He never shared any personal feelings; he dealt in facts and clinical observations. But like a chameleon, he adjusted easily to the tones of the company he kept. He could play with the riffraff, dine with royalty. And yet, I couldn't see where he truly fit into any social order. He was an enigma: You couldn't say that he was charming, and he obviously didn't care if he was perceived to be; he presented an impervious front against how others viewed him. He was direct, and sometimes his directness was seen as condescension by the ignorant or those lacking self-confidence. Here was a superior intellect, a man well-schooled, fabulously wealthy, and well-connected. But all those qualities were in stark contrast against his hulking height and sharp, hawk-like features, with eyes like targets, darkly ringed irises, the color of the sea on an overcast day. I thought that I would never really come to know this man, and I wanted to see who existed beneath the formidable face he showed the world, because Trevor Hunter both fascinated and frightened me.

And here I sat, warm and cozy in Conan Doyle's pants. . . .

I unfolded the handkerchief to blow my nose. A whiff of sandalwood filled the air.

Trevor returned, pushing a drinks trolley, atop which sat a steaming covered dish, plates, utensils, glasses, and an uncorked bottle of red wine. He played waiter, placing a cloth over the tabletop, setting the plates, and, like a competent sommelier, pouring an ounce of wine for me to taste. I laughed and nodded.

"You are spoiling me. I may never leave."

"Oh, you'll leave all right," he said. "But you'll leave in a better state than when I found you reveling in the gutter." He lifted the lid of the chafing dish and I nearly swooned when the aroma of Boeuf Bourguignon penetrated my stuffy nose. I hadn't eaten since a breakfast of toasted day-old bread after my morning shift, and the cup of coffee I'd had at Marie's. Before long the succulent stew restored my body and spirit. My eyes were heavy, and I wanted to close them . . . and I must have dozed off for a while because the next thing I saw when they focused was a silver coffeepot on a tray, the dinner dishes having been ferried away.

"Don't apologize," said Trevor with all seriousness. "Why should you stay alert during my discourse on the migration of *Homo sapiens* during the Paleolithic age two-hundred-thousand years ago?" He smiled, and then chuckled. "Why should you be any different from anybody else? Cigarette?" he offered from an elaborately enameled box, as if to stave off my apologies. "I have these specially blended along with my pipe tobacco and sent from Moreland's in London."

I took a cigarette, and Trevor lit it with the table lighter. I leaned back in my chair, from which I had not moved since I had claimed it—what—an hour ago, two? I looked at the mantel clock. I'd been there for three hours! Probably sleeping for the past two.

Shifting in my chair, I felt a sharp twinge in my back. I wondered if I could ever get out of the chair without burning pain when it came time to go home.

Trevor poured coffee and told me to fix it as I liked it. I stirred in sugar and cream, and a plate was placed before me with a slice of rich chocolate cake. My belly had not been this full for quite some time, but the cake looked luscious. The coffee was a strong, smooth brew, and I wasn't about to pass that up, either.

So when Trevor said, "Now," as he tossed his spent match in the ashtray, I was taken by surprise to hear him say, "I don't think you should continue meeting with those club men."

The fork was halfway to my lips, and stopped suspended there as I watched him draw deeply on the briar. The breath he exhaled was intoxicating. But, now I tried to understand why he wanted to boot me out of the club.

My dismay must have shown, and the blank stare prompted him to elaborate.

"You see, Ernest—or perhaps you don't. . . . Perhaps you haven't noticed what's transpired since you've been absent these past weeks."

I felt a sinking in my stomach. A sharp stab of rejection. Wasn't I good enough to take part in our discussions? I had been the first to bring the men together, so now they had all turned on me? Was Trevor Hunter their emissary? Was that why he had followed me, to tell me the men's decision?

Again, he preempted my thoughts, for he said, "You don't know what I am getting at, do you?"

"Frankly, I don't, Trevor," I said hoarsely, truculence lacing my tone.

I felt weak and miserable, stuffed like a sacrificial lamb. Was all this—fanfare—just a last supper for a condemned man?

For the first time in my life I had made friends, and had experienced the camaraderie of those associations. Not while growing up in the orphanage, not during the scant year I spent in college, nor had I really found my place among the newsmen at the *Herald*. With them I had only really known the fleeting promise of good fellowship. Never before had I had this assemblage of like minds who *understood* the art of creation and the pain that sometimes accompanied it.

That Cherish had come into my life and stayed had been the only light to shine into the darkness of my life. Now, all I could feel was betrayal. And like a vulnerable child, reeling from disappointment, I wanted to cry for my loss.

"As I said, you've been absent for the past—what?—couple of months? What did you notice tonight?"

"Are you saying that I have fallen behind? That I can't keep up with—"

"Don't be a fool! You are a talent greater than all those hacks put together, Ernest. I've read your book, the one you wrote years ago, and it is a fine book, and Niles Pickering didn't do a thing to see it succeed, as he should have done."

There was no transition from my feelings of rejection to the rise of my ego, elated at his good opinion of me, and I must have reddened, because I felt the rush of blood gushing into my head at his praise. I was angry, suddenly, that I should have even cared what this horrid, brilliant man thought of me. But, I discovered in that moment how much I really did care.

"If you believe I am a good writer, then, well, damn you! Why do you want to dismiss me?"

"Are you so thick that you haven't noticed the change?"

"I've noticed that everyone is swimming along, hard at work on their books, and yes, I see the change in Mark and Daniel. They have renewed excitement in their lives.

"Can you suspect why?"

"Well, of course! They are writing again! But, I will begin writing again. Soon! I will—"

"This is not about what you will or will not *write*, Ernest."

"Then . . . what?"

"It's about what you will or *will not do!*"

My agony must have shown in my face, and I rose up suddenly, if painfully, from the chair to face him. His fierce eyes flashed a look of pity as they met mine, and then they softened. I hated him for it, and I loathed myself even more because he had seen something inside of me, something I had for so long tried to keep hidden from everyone as well as myself.

"Ernest," he said my name with a gentle tone, "I'm trying to save you."

"I don't know how being expelled from the club is going to save me. What do you really mean by that?"

"It's the only way," he said with an edge of sadness in his voice, "and you are a man worth saving. It's too late for the others, but not for you. Come with me," he said, touching my shoulder, and then he led the way out into the hall and began the climb up the stairs. I followed him as far as the threshold into the hall, and he turned, addressing my hesitation. "I have to show you something;

something that will explain it all so that you will understand."

I followed Trevor up to the second landing, and then around the hall to the third. On we climbed to the top floor, where Trevor stopped at a door, pulled out his keys, and unlocked it. He pressed a light switch.

I entered a room filled with books and papers and stacks of files that stood in piles a foot high atop file cabinets and tables. A desk in front of the windows was dominated by a typewriter, student lamp, and trays containing papers, magazines, newspapers, pillars of books, and a Pre-Columbian stone carving.

I turned to face Trevor watching me from the doorway, on both sides of which were bookshelves whose contents reached the ceiling.

I eyed the collection, a mad exercise in confusion, thousands of volumes jammed into any available vertical and horizontal space, everything askew and cross-hatched like a crazy quilt. But then I saw that there really was method to the madness. Books were grouped by subject, and each subject was shelved alphabetically. Many of the titles were forensic or physiological in nature, having to do with the commission or investigation of crime. There were books on plants and pharmaceuticals, their uses and abuses, and many sinister-looking anthropological publications, the spines of which denoted that the contents were about diabolical practices in far-off

places around the world—Africa, Asia, the West
Indies, Ancient Egypt. There were books on the
Pharaohs' crimes of matricide, fratricide, patricide—a
family affair of poisons and murder; a history of
the Borgias, scheming Popes, and Vatican scandals;
studies of torture, dismemberment, disembowelment,
self-mutilation, cannibalism, violent sexual practices.
There was an extensive collection on religious dogma
as well as hedonistic practices: Judeo-Christian
executions, the Inquisitions, and Roman blood sport;
voodoo, zombies, vampire lore, premature burial,
American Indian rituals, human sacrifice, and Mayan
brain surgeries. And there were numerous books
on the occult: Satanism—many on the black arts—
exorcism and the Roman Catholic Church, journals
about secret organizations from the Masons, Opus
Dei, and the Knights Templar to Yale University's
Skulls. The *how-to*'s included mummification, the
distilling of toxic plants, embalming techniques in
the ancient world, animal dissection, and taxidermy.

"You can peruse the books at another time.
What I want you to see is in here," said Trevor,
walking toward a small alcove through which a door
led into an adjoining room. I followed with curiosity,
my interest piqued as he entered the inner sanctum
and hit the light switch.

"Bulb burnt out," he said, moving onward into
the dark. "Wait a minute while I throw some light
on things."

I heard the spring of a cord chain, and the room became a vision of bouncing orbs and shadows as a shaded work-light lit the room. A serpent-like figure shifted with life, until Trevor steadied the shade. The serpent proved nothing more deadly than a swan's-neck glass retort firmly planted on a refractory table alongside dozens of laboratory apparatuses. Petri dishes, test tubes, bulbous retorts, small and gigantic, glass pipettes, Bunsen burners, funnels, condensers, beakers, and a maze of pipes lined the long steel-topped table at the center of the room.

"My laboratory," Trevor announced, a touch of pride in his voice. "On par with Dr. Gettler's lab, according to our city's great forensic toxicologist."

I'd heard about the famous Dr. Alexander Gettler. He was the first of his kind in the development of testing for the detection of poisons, and had assisted the Chief Medical Examiner of New York City, Dr. Charles Norris, in the investigations for the causes of many suspicious deaths over the past decade.

Trevor threw another switch and more light fell upon on the contents of the room. My attention was drawn to the wall above a sink, on which shelves and cabinets were stocked with vials and tins displaying skull-and-crossbones labeling alongside everyday household cleaners and medical remedies. These were presented in neatly labeled classifications according to their individual properties. There were everyday household products as well: Radium Spray—Bug Killer, Disinfectant and Furniture Polish, Burnett's Cocaine, Fowler's Solution—commonly used by women to whiten their skin—which was placed beside Rat Poison, both products containing arsenic.

I suppose my expression of wonder was what prompted Trevor to reach for his keys. "That's cantharidin," he said after unlocking the glass-paneled cabinet door, "commonly known as Spanish Fly . . . calalar beans. . . ." He removed the green glass bottle to show me as he continued.

"Used by African witch doctors." Picking out another, "Here's *Tinctura gelsemii*, made from the root of yellow jasmine. These are a few selections from my pharmacopeia of lethal concoctions."

"So it appears," I said with a sense of macabre wonder.

"*Bacillus anthracis*," continued Trevor, matter-of-factly as he moved along. "A smidgeon of that will definitely put an end to your party plans; belladonna—you might know it as Deadly Nightshade—or Devil's Berries or Death Cherries."

He pointed, now: "Black walnut, Bulgarian umbrella, catuwoba, and coline—made from hemlock. Curare . . . datura!

Trevor became more animated and his voice held an edge of excitement as he continued.

"Mandragora! Mescaline! Monkshood! You know, Ernest, in old times monkshood was used in an attempt to kill werewolves. Tricky, though; you need a full moon and it is damn near impossible getting a werewolf to take his medicine, you know?" he chuckled.

He opened another cabinet and removed a bottle, which he cradled in his hand.

"Here's morphine . . . kills pain—forever, if too much is administered; otherwise, good for what ails you." He returned the bottle to its place, and then pointed to "nitro benzene, phosphorus, *hmmm*, yes, phosphorus can put an end to all your problems . . . potassium cyanide, used as a fixer in the photographer's darkroom since the 1860s, a dangerous chemical to have on hand. Easy to procure. There's a famous murder case—but that is for another time.

"Stropanthus, yes, one would need stropanthus for one's arrow quivers," he chuckled. "Strychnine—paralyzes the victim first. Tansy! And here's thallium. First you lose your hair and then you lose your life. Agatha Christie likes thallium—for her books, that is. I recall we discussed thallium at Tony's birthday last winter. Quite unpleasant stuff."

"Trevor," I said, in an attempt to stop the poisonous inventory, "why do you keep these dreadful things?"

"For my work, of course!" Seeing the horror in my face, he let out with a loud cackle. "Don't be an ass, Stringer! I'm a scientist. I don't go around poisoning people no matter how much I dislike them.

And considering my general view of my fellow man, there'd be few left standing.

"I keep these pharmaceuticals for the purpose of experimentation in order to detect, in human and animal tissue samples, the presence of a murderer's lethal poison. These things have always proved difficult to isolate, you know. For instance, Dr. Gettler has performed thousands of tests in his laboratory for the detection of cyanide in the blood and organs of a victim. And then there was the problem of potassium chloride.... Illusive, for some time it was deemed undetectable! Let me explain why:

"After death, there is a natural rise in the potassium levels in the blood, due to the start of decomposition. Decomposing cells give off potassium, you see. Now, if a murderer injects his victim with a solution of potassium chloride, which is certainly deadly, and a number of hours pass before the body is discovered, thereby causing a delay in the toxicology tests, the poison will be disguised. The trick is to discover a method that will uncover the poison. This is what I do. I am, alongside others, trying to solve the mysteries behind heinous crimes.

"Take the dilemma of hydrogen cyanide gas, used to fumigate rats and other pests. Gettler was able to show, in the Jackson Case back in '22, that there were greater levels of hydrogen cyanide in the lungs than would naturally appear through decomposition. Thus, a murderer was convicted on Dr. Gettler's toxicological evidence!

"Sad to say, but an easy method—if you wanted someone dead—would be to stand him for a drink of rotgut at any number of questionable speaks around town. Your victim would die within a week of imbibing the methanol these bootleggers are passing off for whiskey. Your victim would be just one of thousands suffering miserable deaths each year since the country went dry, and you, the murderer, would suffer no fear of discovery!"

I was speechless.

"You should be flattered, Ernest. Only a few people have ever been invited here. And from our club, just Tony. It should prove to you that I don't think of you as the murdering kind."

"I suppose I should be flattered at your high opinion of me. Or, is it that I shouldn't be writing mysteries, is that what you're saying?"

"I should think not. Come around here," he said, reaching for my elbow. "This is what I want you to look at and then consider carefully what you see."

He brought me over to face the opposite long wall of the room. The entire surface was covered with news clippings and forensic reports tacked on boards, and what appeared to be evidentiary findings from dozens of murder cases. It would take time to unravel all that these postings meant, and what discoveries they would eventually lead to. I turned to look at Trevor.

"News clippings?" I said. "Are these cases you have an interest in, toxicologically speaking?"

Seeing my confusion, he pointed to a news clipping dated Monday of the previous week. It was a headline from the *Detroit Register*:

The Trial of Mary Connelly Begins Today

I read aloud: "*. . . on trial for the poisoning murder of her husband, Martin Connelly, last June—*"

Below was an obituary column for the allegedly poisoned Martin Howard Connelly cut out from a June edition of the same newspaper. I saw that the date of Connolly's birth was underlined: *February 6, 1889.*

"All right, Trevor. Have you had a part in solving this case?"

"It's not about me." Then he pointed to another clipping alongside the Mary Connolly trial announcement.

Cut from the August 10, 1929, *Boston Globe* was an obituary for Richard Hartley Hayes, engineer. I began to read aloud the first column:

"*Born June 7, 1889, in Worchester, Massachusetts. . . . Tufts University, leaves behind his wife of fifteen years, Esther Wright Hayes; one son, Robert Hartley Hayes, numerous cousins—what's* this got to do—?"

"Just remember the man's name. Remember the date of his birth and the date of his death," said Trevor. Then he pointed to the *Daily News* headline announcing the suicide of Frederick Feldman, the writer who had supposedly stolen Daniel Cousins' novel.

"Yes, I know about this. But, what does this have to do with anything? I don't understand."

"Feldman may have hung, but he was poisoned first."

"Not suicide?"

"You are beginning to catch on."

"Well, you are saying he was murdered. A man who takes poison doesn't then go off and hang himself."

"That's right," nodded Trevor. And then: "Considering the events of yesterday ..."

"Yesterday? What am I missing?"

Haven't you seen today's papers?"

"I haven't had time."

Trevor retrieved today's newspaper, the *Herald Tribune*, turning to page four. I looked at the copy above the photograph of a man I recognized, one taken in better days. I read aloud: *"Publishing Mogul James Morrow was found dead last night in his sprawling Park Avenue apartment.* Oh ... my God!"

"When I saw this, I called Dr. Norris—our city's Chief Medical Examiner. He told me the death initially appeared to be suicide, and that Alexander Gettler was doing the toxicology to determine the suspected agent, cyanide. So I called Alex, and he told me that he did indeed determine the cause of death to be cyanide poisoning. He referred to a suicide note near the body in which Morrow confessed his guilt for the murder of Frederick Feldman."

"Holy crap," was all I could say, and then the thought that followed: "Jim Morrow killed his lover, and then because he figured the cops were closing in, he killed himself!"

"One of many possible hypotheses. On the contrary, Morrow had never been a suspect in his lover's murder. At the time of the murder, Morrow was in Europe with his wife and daughter. And as you see in the paper, there's no mention of any suicide note confessing to anything found on or near Morrow."

"But, you said—"

"Gettler and Norris never actually saw the note; Norris explained that its discovery was mentioned by the coroner who arrived at the scene to examine the body. Morrow was found lying face-down on the floor of his study. When the coroner turned over the body, he discovered a note crumpled in Morrow's fist. According to him, it was a typewritten note, two short sentences, in which Morrow confesses to murdering Feldman, and asks forgiveness from his family. The detective on the scene retrieved it. Interesting that there is no such suicide confession in the evidence locker as of this afternoon."

"You think somebody—"

"Of course. Need to spare the survivors from the pain and embarrassment."

"But, if the coroner saw it, read it—"

"Ernest, the Office of the Chief Medical Examiner reports its forensic findings to the New York City Police Department, that's all it does. Unless physical evidence gathered by the police is handed over to Gettler's lab for analysis, it is boxed as evidence. No such letter made it to the evidence room at the precinct. Morrow's widow is, after all, the niece of our city's esteemed police commissioner, and it's all about protecting the family from scandal."

"How can they cover this up? There will be an inquest."

"The Morrows are wealthy and money can make lots of troublesome things disappear. Anyway, the consensus is what would be the good of exposing the truth? Both men are dead. The admission that Morrow killed Feldman closes the Feldman case at last. That Feldman and Morrow were homosexuals is moot. The officers on the scene will undoubtedly be promoted and monetarily compensated, mark my words. To rest my case, just look at tonight's newspapers: suicide, yes; Morrow's connection with the murder of his lover, not mentioned. Alexander Gettler and Dr. Norris are above reproach, and having eliminated natural causes will declare

Morrow's death by cyanide poisoning. The police will argue suicide, not murder, at the inquest, rest assured. End of story."

"*Ohhh,*" I sighed.

"What is it?"

"Daniel. . . . I mean, he looked good this evening, happier than I'd ever—I wonder why he didn't mention—Trevor, he doesn't know about it!"

"Sure he does. I think he had a hand in it."

The accusation stunned me. "He'd never—Morrow's confession and suicide was the result of his guilt and shame."

"What? Don't you think Daniel capable of murder?"

"Certainly not! He talks a good game of revenge, but to commit such an act? Never! Just because he detested these men for what they did to him, doesn't mean he would do anything like you're suggesting. They were bad people, not because of their illicit relationship, but for what they took from Daniel."

"That's to be determined. What about blackmail?"

"You've got to be kidding! Daniel's mother built a fortune, which he will inherit. He even kept his job at the *Post* to keep independent."

"One doesn't have to *need* money to blackmail a fellow, you know."

"What evidence is there?"

"There isn't any evidence . . . yet. But he had motive—a strong, brooding hatred. And as you just said, you'd never seen him as happy as he was tonight. And there is this, Ernest . . ."

My sinuses were throbbing. I was exhausted from a long day, the effects of dinner and wine and cognac, aching from my fall, and the mental calisthenics Trevor was putting me through. Mostly, I was feeling a deep distrust of the motives of this man.

"I see you are in pain. The sinuses?" asked Trevor, and without waiting for a reply, he turned and walked around to a row of his cabinets.

He studied the various vials and tins, and then made selections. From a drawer, he brought out a small funnel, and then, all items gathered at the sink counter, he began extracting from each vial bottle, using a glass dropper, their liquids and then transferring them into a small glass beaker. Satisfied, he swirled it all about, sniffed the results, and then poured the contents through the funnel into a brown-glass bottle. Screwing on the dropper cap, he walked over to me and said, "Here's a remedy for your sinuses, Ernest. It's a homeopathic preparation of natural oils in a suspension that my father developed years ago."

Then, back to the tins, he began to measure scoopfuls of dried herbs into a bowl. "Tomorrow I will have prepared for you a tincture of lungwort, coltsfoot, lobelia, and horehound to soothe those mucous membranes. Oh, I know the ingredients sound diabolical, but the result is effective, Ernest. For now, try the drops. One drop in each nostril should help immediately."

Trevor watched me with expectancy from behind the long laboratory table. I met his eyes, trying to discern his real intent. I figured that if Trevor wanted to kill rather than cure me he wouldn't have wasted time showing me his lab. Hell, he could have done me in with any number of lethal liquids he had on hand, dosed in my cognac. And he could have done me in on the parlor floor, rolled me down the cellar stars and buried me in the basement, rather than having to drag my dead corpse down three flights of stairs.

I was really over-thinking things, getting paranoid. I did as told, and remarkably, in seconds I felt my sinuses cool. I smiled and he smiled back.

"Feeling better? Good. Let's go downstairs. I have more to tell you."

"Can't it wait? I mean, I'm spent. I have to be out by four o'clock to make the bakery deliveries."

"Well," he said, shutting the lights as we made our way out of the laboratory. "I really don't think this can wait until you're well rested."

He locked the door to the laboratory, and then once in the hall, the door to the study. We descended silently to the parlor floor, Trevor taking the lead.

Chapter Four

"Please," he said, as I loitered in the hall. "This can't wait. I fear you will be approached, and there are things you need to know, and things we need to plan."

His hand swept an invitation for me to return to my place by the fire. The room was dimly lit by a lamp near the bay left on when we had retreated upstairs, and the fire was dwindling. He switched on another table lamp whose light was swallowed up into the dark corners of the room, and then threw another log on the grate.

I took my seat, the words *I fear you will be approached*, swirling through my head.

Things I needed to know. . . .

Things we need to plan. . . .

The nebulousness of the comments was weighted with foreboding. As a new round of rain-showers lashed at the windows, and the wind whistled and echoed down through the chimney, apprehension chased away my exhaustion.

Flames caught the dry wood like eager fingers; a draft sent sparks flying like fireflies up the chimney after a herald of crackles. Shadows flitted along the walls and ceiling like ghostly dancers. Through the darkened windowpanes, I watched the chestnut tree near the curb shaking its remaining leaves frantically, a futile distress signal.

I leaned back in the wingchair, my brow turned toward the welcomed warmth, as Trevor stamped out an errant ember that had threatened the parquet, before returning the hearth screen.

Without a word that might express my wariness, I watched him closely, and observed his measured movements. I could almost see his analytical mind working, sensed that he was carefully gathering his words, determining his approach to revealing something important, perhaps even unpleasant; all the while he poured snifters of cognac, handed me one, and then went about the ritual packing of his pipe with the fragrant tobacco from the humidor beside his chair.

When I failed to speak, to respond as he had probably hoped I would to his last remark, his eyes leveled on mine for a long moment. Then, in what seemed an incongruous statement, he said:

"Do you remember a conversation we had back last summer? We were outside at Marie's. It was that unbearably hot evening when Stephen Shaw appeared from his hiding place to interrupt our talk?"

"He was a real pleasure."

"Yes!" laughed Trevor.

"I've never known a more disagreeable son-of-a-bitch. I wish he had no part of our group. I don't know why you and Anthony allow it. The other men . . . Mark and Daniel, they are not in love with him."

"Yes, I know. But at times, as repugnant as he can be, he does add another perspective to our points of view, doesn't he? And, he doesn't kowtow to Tony."

"It's the other way around, isn't it? I remember when I was out with Tony that time, oh, a year or so ago, at that speak down the street from Marie's, and you and Shaw came in, stood at the bar, and when you came over to say hello to Tony, the brute came over, too, and he pretty much accosted Tony with all sorts of vile insinuations. I was surprised that a man of your standing had befriended a creep like Shaw."

"I am not his friend. He is of no consequence to me. He latched onto me when we had crossed paths at . . . a place I sometimes frequent. He is simply a cretin stuck in an age of cultural sophistication. But, although I am tolerant of most people, I am certainly not his friend. However, Stephen Shaw has the uncanny knack of looking into a person and *seeing* things that most other human beings are blind to. He has what Hemingway refers to as a built-in shit detector."

"I suppose . . ."

"And he uses that ability to wrangle out of his quarry certain truths. Truths that are often best kept hidden."

"Blackmail? Are you saying that Shaw is a blackmailer?"

"In a way. An emotional blackmailer, and he does it for kicks. I certainly doubt it involves exchanging cash."

I said, "Tonight, after a long time, he started riding Anthony again. He gets such pleasure from being cruel. Why in God's name does Anthony stand it, since it upsets him so much that he stormed out with his lame excuses before our talk had started?"

"Shaw knows something about Tony that Tony wishes to have remain secret. I first suspected it last summer in the courtyard. Their acrimony reached far beyond mutual dislike."

I recalled chalking up Shaw's words as nothing more than a vitriolic attack on Anthony's ambiguous sexuality. The thought had crossed my mind on several occasions that Anthony Young, in spite of his popularity with his female readers, was in fact less than successful in relationships with the opposite sex. At times I thought he might suffer from impotence or that he was homosexual.

"The comment about rape?" I said. "I remember. Shaw was baiting him that he wasn't manly enough to 'get it up,' don't you think?"

"That's what I thought. *At first*," said Trevor. "But there were more little comments, and Tony would not always react in a way one would expect from him. Tony has a sharp wit, and a retort is his usual defense against idiotic taunts. But, Shaw effectively *unravels* the man."

We locked eyes for a moment. I couldn't read him. Was it sadness that I saw in his eyes? And loss?

"You and Tony have been friends for a long time," I said.

"Yes," he said, nodding. And then with a chortle he added, "Aside from his rather persnickety ways, he complements my often supercilious nature."

This self-effacing admission made me smile. I watched him in the firelight, those angular features softened; it was a sentimental aspect of Trevor Hunter I'd not seen before.

"I've always held firm the belief that one should not ask a question one is not prepared to know the answer to. In most cases, the truth will set us free. But there are times when unmasking a truth can become a tremendous burden and a test of our scruples. But, given the opportunity, even if the opportunity is serendipitously offered, my curiosity will always win out. What I discovered, and what I am about to tell you, is disturbing. But as I said before, *I am trying to save you*."

"Trevor, will you just tell me what this is all about? You have my full attention."

"After Shaw's appearance in the courtyard last year, I dismissed his comment as a show of bravado. He has always behaved audaciously. I suppose it gets him the attention he needs. So, I thought of it as nothing more than Shaw being Shaw. I filed the incident away in the nether regions of my mind for a more pressing matter that concerned me that summer, the task of assisting in the classification of fibers at Dr. Gettler's laboratory. I thought nothing more about it.

"And then, last winter, I accepted an invitation from an old school chum, Michael Reddington, with whom I had shared rooms at Oxford. In town from Boston, he was staying at the Harvard Club—his medical degree is from Harvard—so we had dinner there. He had also invited a friend from that university to join us, a specialist in endocrinology, practicing in Detroit and in town while attending a medical conference.

"Our discussion was little more than an exchange of reminiscences from college days, and we talked about the opera season, about the new jazz. It was certainly not a meeting of doctors conferring on new developments in our fields. So, when the two friends spoke fondly of their days at Harvard, I found my thoughts drifting away from their exchange as I had not attended that good school.

"But, when the endocrinologist mentioned the measles outbreak at Harvard in 1912, which sent many students to hospital, I remembered Tony telling me that he had had to leave school because he had fallen ill during the epidemic. Complications had set in, and Tony said he had missed his last two semesters while recuperating from home. Now, Tony's degree is from Princeton, class of 1914. That's something we must note before I continue, because there was no outbreak of measles at Princeton.

"I said to my friend, Michael, 'I know a chap who had so been infected.'"

"'So many were that year at Harvard!' said Michael's friend.

"Michael said, 'Yes, and the outbreak came only a week or so after the big scandal.'

"'Oh, right!' said Michael's friend, 'That was all rumor, don't you think?'

"'I think there was a grain of truth to it. There always is some truth behind a rumor,' said Michael.

"'A school prank gone wrong, I'll bet,' insisted his friend.

"Aware that I was lost, Michael turned to his friend and asked: 'Four—or was it five?—'

"'Five. There were the four who were expelled, and their victim.'

" 'The victim's name?' asked Michael.

" 'Don't remember that.'

"And then Michael's friend began to pull memories from his head: 'You know, the pudgy boy who directed the Greek play? He remembered him because he was in The Pudding's *The Crystal Gazer* and wore a toga. Lost the sheet when Jimmy Russell—remember Jimmy? Little fellow, big feet?—when Jimmy's sword caught on it. Tore the house down! Poor guy....'

"And then he leaped to memories of Robert Benchley. 'Benchley—remember when Robert Benchley—well the fellow I'm talking about, the one lost his sheet, was reciting the Anthony speech from Julius Caesar—'

"'Eureka!' said Michael. 'That's it! His name was Anthony. Anthony . . . something or other . . .'

"'Youngston' said the friend. 'Right you are, old sport! Anthony Youngston,' said Michael. 'I always felt a little sorry for the kid, and not just for the dropped-sheet incident.'

"Since I had an opening, I asked, 'Why is that?'

"Michael thought for a moment and said, 'He was an odd sort, never really fit in, know what I mean? Terribly bright, I thought, until I realized he always had to show off what he knew in order to distract from all that he did *not* know. You know the sort. Perfect target, the butt of many jokes, pranks; he bore it all well, got through them, I thought.'

"'Well, they went too far. A prank gone haywire,' said the friend.

"I asked if it had to do with a fraternity hazing, but they both said it wasn't. It wasn't a prank, it was an *assault*.

"Michael said, 'The fellows who did it were expelled, remember? Led by a football player, a tight end. His name was Connolly.'"

I must have made a gasp of surprise, because Trevor paused in his retelling.

"'Youngston never returned to school,' they said, and I asked, 'What terrible thing did they do to this Youngston fellow?' To which Michael replied, 'He was stripped and attacked, in a personal way.'

"'*They sodomized him?*' I asked, and was told that *that* was the rumor, but, before the rumor had time to pick up speed, nearly a quarter of the student body fell ill. Classes were canceled for several weeks, and then came time for final exams, graduation. Anthony and his tormenters were gone from the school by then. Out of sight, out of mind.

"I asked if they recalled the names of the other expelled boys. It was a matter of connecting the dots, so to speak, from one little remembrance to the next. It seems that the fellow Connolly shared rooms with a chap named Rudy Valentine. Michael's friend remembers that name, because when the Italian Valentino struck it big in the pictures, he remembered the Harvard Rudy, who was a big, handsome blond boy, like the guy in the Arrow shirt advertisements, the antithesis of the Italian *Sheik*.

"'Killed in the war, was Rudy,' said Michael. His friend hadn't heard.

"Michael added, 'There was that other one. The one they called 'The Masher.'

"'A pugilist built like a bull with the face of an angel.'

"Michael's friend couldn't recall the name of the boy. Of course, the obvious was staring at us. I said, 'Gentlemen, we're sitting here of all places, at the Harvard Club. Let's go look at the class photographs. Since none of the men graduated, we'll need to find them in the 1911 junior year student body pictures, if not certainly on the Crimson team pix.'

"After coffee and cigars, we searched out the team photographs."

"And you found the other two?" I asked.

Trevor nodded.

"And one of the attackers was named Hayes?"

"Yes. Otherwise known as 'The Masher.'"

"What about the fourth man?"

"Ronald Millington the Third, heir to the Millington Textile fortune, killed in the war."

Trevor got up and went over to a writing desk, pulled open a drawer, and took out a writing pad and pencil. He walked back to his chair and began writing.

When he had finished he handed the pad to me. There were our names listed vertically down the left side of the page, beginning with Anthony's. An arrow extended to point to the names of those murdered: Connolly and Hayes, the dates of their demise in ascending order. Next on the club list was Daniel. Again, Trevor had drawn an arrow to the right and listed the names Feldman and Morrow, adding dates of death beside their names.

"The arrows are the connectors, Ernest. The dates show that Tony started the ball rolling. Then came Daniel's victims. So, it suggests that you and, or, Mark Wendt are next. For God's sake, Ernest, the man who ran down Mark's girlfriend. The bootlegger! He's probably next to die, unless you and Tony made a plan to kill Harvey Price, your nemesis, which I trust has not happened—yet. But, with Tony the ringleader, I believe he will approach you and try to feel you out."

"Oh, this is fucking crazy!"

"Yes, it is crazy. Actually, it is insane," said Trevor.

"The distance of time . . ."

"What was that?"

I replayed the words Anthony Young had spoken just a few hours before: *It is the distance in time that can make all the difference, especially if you have had no contact with your intended victim, no dealings whatsoever over the years, so that you are never even remotely considered a suspect in his murder.*

"Yes, that was Tony's theory. And the timing of the murders of his Harvard attackers fit. But there is a second qualification necessary for the perfect murder, remember? 'The most important element that secures you from being caught is if your victim has never dared admit to, or told about, his crime to another living soul.'"

I finished the statement: "'There would be no motive against you, because your victim was never culpable for having committed a crime for which you sought revenge.' He's committed the perfect murders," I whispered.

"Not so perfect."

"Oh, you mean that Shaw knows."

"I doubt he does. But he does, however, possess a talent for disseminating his suspicions, whether based on fact or not. He relishes causing trouble. I suspect, because of his constant goading and insinuations, that Shaw sensed that Tony had been the victim of some sort of violence or injustice, that Tony had a secret. It's possible that Shaw may have heard an old rumor. But I doubt he knows about the Connolly and Hayes murders. Or that Tony did anything other than to write a fiction novel employing an imagined theory he voiced to us all about the perfect crime. He'd never believe Tony capable of violence. He's always calling him a pussy-boy behind his back."

"I find it almost impossible to believe any of this, knowing Anthony as I do."

"Ernest, when are you going to realize that we never know what is in another person's mind, in his heart, what desperate need, what *torment* drives one to such lengths to discard one's morality in order to ease a nagging pain. We never know what another human being is capable of. My God! We rarely know *ourselves*, what *we* are capable of, until we face a crisis of faith or courage."

I reflected on his words, his adamant appeal.

Anthony Young. A murderer.

And then it all seemed to come together in my mind; everything else began to fall into place. *Daniel*

Cousins. . . . I spoke his name aloud, a whisper, really, and almost regretted that I had. I dreaded the words that Trevor would speak in reply.

But Trevor said nothing, just rose from his chair and emptied the bowl of his pipe in the fireplace. The coals hissed. The wind had subsided and the worst of the storm had passed. A fire truck's bell clanged in the distance, somewhere near Fifth Avenue.

"You've been absent from the meetings these past months."

"You know why."

"It's a good thing."

"Why did you say you wanted to save me? Do you think I would discard my morality for the thrill of revenge? Revenge on Harvey Price?"

"Ernest, forgive me, but, you see, I know about the past. What you endured as a child, witnessing the atrocity of your mother's murder."

When I shot up from my chair, he touched my shoulder. "Please! Let me continue. I know, too, that you have suffered certain injustices, and that you are a man of moral character. If you ask how I know this, I will tell you that I have read your work. An artist's work is an excellent measure of a man, a glimpse into the creator's soul. An author's words tell a lot: whether he has integrity, whether he is a man of courage and honesty. One can't fail to see that you possess those fine qualities.

"The others—Daniel, Mark, Tony—all narcissists."

I objected, but Trevor pressed on.

"Yes, they are, no matter how much they appear otherwise, how much enjoyment you may find in their company. Many narcissists have personality disorders. Some are sociopaths, some, psychopaths, but they are often viewed as very charming people. Like Anthony."

In one full sweep, I had lost faith in the men I had come to trust and care for, men I had come to believe were the only real friends I had ever known.

"Look at the men as I have seen them: They all seethe with resentment, and their anger burns through; you can see it, feel it. Each believes he has been victimized to some degree, and perhaps that is true. Who hasn't known some degree of injustice and deceit? You, however, who have suffered the worst, have struggled the most, are pure at heart. I know this, too, because of Cherish."

I reeled as I was shifted from abject disbelief of his assessment of my friends to embarrassment as he praised my character, and then I was plunged into red-hot fury at his mention of my woman.

"What do you know about her? What does she have to do with anything?"

"I'm sorry if you are angry. I won't mention her again. I mean only to help. Let me just say that your love for her is *admirable*, Ernest!"

"She is everything to me!"

"And that is dedication."

I was near tears, on the brink of hysteria, and wanted to bolt out of the house, home to my love, never to see again this man who was systematically tearing my life apart one step at a time. And what was he insinuating about Cherish? I wanted to know.

But, I didn't ask. I couldn't. Whether or not his touch hypnotized me, I don't know, but when he touched my shoulder, I felt compassion in his firm touch, and I resumed my place by the dwindling fire and dashed back the dregs of brandy left in my glass.

"I don't want to talk about her," I said, decisively.

The grandfather clock in the hall struck the hour. I found myself counting off the chimes in my head, while Trevor went to the window bay, his back fully turned toward me, to look out through the swag draperies at the street. Midnight. I knew he was giving me time to regain my composure before the next round of revelations. I sensed—I *knew* there was more to come.

.

Chapter Five

The next morning, I tried to maintain a semblance of my normal routine. Somehow I managed to appear at the bakery at the usual early hour to fulfill the deliveries on my morning route. By ten o'clock, I was in such a severe state from lifting stock onto and off the truck that my boss, who is a strict but kind-natured man, asked what was the matter with me. I explained that I had fallen the night before, and when he lifted my shirt he whistled at the bruise that had spread along my side. I hobbled home, told that I should stay there for the rest of the week, and that someone would cover my route until I returned. The kindness was intended to console, but I felt weakened by it. Upon my return home, I took the draft that Trevor had given me before I left in the early hours of the morning. It contained a powerful pain reliever, and I slept through the day into the night and through the next morning.

When I awoke, Cherish was there, standing tentatively over me as I lay in the bed, a steaming cup of coffee in her hand, a smile to warm me even more. For a moment I had forgotten my injury; when I tried to raise myself on my elbow, a sharp stab reminded me.

"You really did it, my poor darling," she said, tucking a pillow under my back. "You've slept around the clock—twice around the clock."

There was no position that suited me, but the sharp pain finally settled into a nagging ache while I sipped from the cup she handed me.

"You've had visitors." My blank response prompted her to say, "That man, Travis—I mean Trevor, one of your book club friends—stopped by last night. He told me all about your fall during the storm. Why didn't you wake me when you got in?"

"It was awfully late and I—"

"Your friend, Trevor, is quite funny, giving me instructions on how to brew your tea—it's some medicine for your sinuses. He brought it with him. And then he said to make sure that you take this other medicine," she held up a brown glass bottle on the nightstand, "when you wake up— only one teaspoon of this every six hours, for pain. He said there is no point wrapping the ribs. After examining you the other night, he says you are just badly bruised."

"When exactly was he here? Why didn't you wake me?"

"I don't know. Early last night, and he told me not to disturb you. He just wanted to see that you were all right. Oh, and he told me to give you this," she said, handing me an envelope.

I placed it under the covers to read when I was alone.

"You are becoming very popular, darling, because then you had another visitor last night. Funny little man . . . Anthony Young? I told him you had hurt yourself, and he said he knew, because that man, Trevor, had telephoned him about it. He was very upset for you. He came to offer any help we needed. I thought that was a rather nice gesture, even though I couldn't think of a thing he could do. But, listen to this, here's the best part. He asked to see my collection of paintings, and wouldn't you know—he bought two!"

"Anthony Young bought *two* of your paintings?"

"That's what I just said, silly! Don't look so shocked! Why? Is he a collector or something? Somebody important?" she started to gush, her eyes sparkling, not only from the sun pouring in through the window, but because the long-dormant hope of her dreams becoming fulfilled was once again rising. "I mean, I thought he must be somebody important, so I brought him up to the studio. He met Carlos, too. And he said he wanted to introduce me to some people he knew—"

I wasn't hearing the rest of what she was saying. I was too upset that the man who may have murdered two men and possibly mentored, and maybe even helped, Daniel in the execution of another two, had managed to worm his way into my home, and then charmingly finagled his way into my wife's good graces with purchases of her artworks and suggestions of influencing her successful future.

I needed to get up; I felt so trapped and ineffectual lying in my bed. My mind frantically searched for a plan, something I could do to keep Anthony away without raising his suspicions of my mistrust. I started to get out of bed to head for the toilet. Trevor's letter fell to the floor. Cherish retrieved it, and before I could take it from her, she ripped open the flap and pulled out the note card. I stood frozen as she read, fearing what message it might contain.

"Nice," she said at last. "Nice that he is so concerned."

"May I read my letter, now?"

She handed it to me, waiting, as I opened the embossed, heavy-stock note card and perused the strong, long strokes of black penmanship.

"Yes, Trevor is a very nice man," I said with a sigh after reading the innocuous lines, *Hope you are feeling better, and will stop in tomorrow evening.*

I shaved while Cherish ran a hot bath, in which I lingered for some time, thinking things over, not resolved in any way on what was best for me to do about Anthony Young and Daniel Cousins. Eventually, Cherish stuck her head around the door to say there was some leftover spaghetti she'd warmed up in the frying pan, which she would set out for me, since I had to be starving after sleeping so long. She was going uptown to Neysa's to pose for an illustrated cover of *Cosmopolitan*. Something to do with the new styles of hats. Neysa would be drawing and painting while at the same time entertaining her celebrity friends, who, by open and ongoing invitation seven days a week, would climb the flights to her studio to join dozens of other notables crammed in to shoot the breeze, gossip, and promote themselves until they scattered off for dinner or the theatre or whatever these people actually do. It was the way of life for the successful illustrator, and Cherish would, no doubt, enjoy the company of actors and writers and no-accounts, chugging down bathtub gin and plates of chop suey from the Chinese joint down the street while she sat with a new-styled hat propped atop her head. I used to sometimes go with her, because I like Neysa McMein, and some of those who dropped in were interesting people. But after a time, I found the general tone of the constant cocktail party and the exaggerated exuberance of its participants wearing on my nerves. Everybody seemed to be trying too hard, too hard to sound witty, too hard to have fun.

Cherish pecked my cheek and was gone, leaving me to a plate of reheated spaghetti.

On the evening of Anthony's dinner at Delmonico's in celebration of the sale of his new book, at Cherish's insistence, I got into a cab to take me from the apartment to the restaurant. Anthony had paid a tidy sum for the two paintings, far more than I could earn in several months. So, I acquiesced. I could not return to my job—I could hardly throw up a sticky window sash in the apartment let alone load and unload trays without spasms that nearly brought me to my knees. A week after my fall, I was in as much pain as I had been the day it happened. Trevor warned me it might take a few weeks before the sharp stabbing pain subsided into a dull ache. To cough or sneeze or bend was pure agony.

As the cab passed City Hall in the approach to the Financial District, the traffic grew unusually heavy for that time of the evening. Ordinarily, by seven p.m. the streets and sidewalks around the Financial District are pretty much free of frenetic pedestrian and automobile traffic.

I have imagined that the hyperactivity of all the trading and banking and the mania of speculation whirls wildly about and forms a vortex emanating from somewhere beneath the Federal Reserve Bank and Stock Exchanges and spirals out with an ineffable force spreading its energy to the outer regions of our city. It originates here, that sense of power and urgency, from these granite cathedrals of finance and commerce. I sometimes think it is accountable for the quickened pace on which New Yorkers seem to thrive.

But, tonight, the streets were crammed with vehicles, with downtrodden-looking men loitering about in groups before the great brass doors of brokerage houses and banking institutions and alongside newsstands. There was a chilling, funereal pall spread over the landscape, like mourners after the church service waiting for the casket to come out.

A newsy was hawking the stack of late editions tucked under his arm, and his customers were diminishing his supply, I could see, as we stood stuck in the cross-traffic at Broadway and Dey Street. I rolled down my window in an effort to catch the drift of the news story that was causing the activity, and hearing nothing, I yelled over to a fellow near the curb at the corner, "What's happening?"

"The sky caved in," he shouted back before continuing on his way.

I caught sight of the headline from a newspaper discarded in the street below my window:

Stock Prices Fall $14,000,000,000 in Massive Selloff to Unload Stocks

It had all begun last week, last Thursday, I remembered reading about it, and many of the little traders were wiped out then. But, there were assurances that stocks would rally, that the Federal Reserve would cut interest rates. Tonight, I didn't need a newspaper to tell me that efforts to stave off a catastrophe had been futile; all I had to do was to look at the dispirited faces of the men in the street.

As the taxi pulled up to the curved, triangular building that marked the corner where Beaver Street met William Street, I left the Wall Street calamity behind me as my thoughts were pulled back to the terrifying prospects that awaited me behind the etched-glass doors of the restaurant if I did not play my part right. I felt a sinking in my gut.

The one and only time I'd ever been to Delmonico's was when I was a boy, four or five years old. It was a celebration of some kind, but I don't remember what about. It was all impression: My mother wore a dress that shined blue and then green when she moved, and rustled like crisp sheets of paper rubbing together. I had never seen her dressed up so fancily. She was very beautiful. I felt very grown up to be at the restaurant and surrounded by grownups. I was wearing my new royal-blue velvet suit with knickers and a matching sailor cap. I remember the words Mother used to describe it: *royal blue*. "Like *Blue Boy*," she'd say. "Where's my little Blue Boy?" she'd say. I was an adult before I understood that she was referring to the portrait by Gainsborough. I remember the big starched collar chafing my neck.

My father was in evening clothes, as were all the men at our table. There were oysters, plates and plates of them, and it was the first time I had tasted such a thing, pinkish-gray and convoluted on their oddly shaped little dishes. They looked disgusting, but I wanted to try one, to be like the grownups, and nearly choked when I bit into the slimy thing and it squirted and everybody laughed. I've never had oysters since.

There was music, too. Not the kind of loud, throbbing stuff that quaked through my body in the big holiday parades, but lighthearted fare played by gentlemen in evening clothes who were seated, not marching.

I remember a man who was dark and very tall and thin, with a pencil moustache, and I think he was a friend of my father's. My mother was always particularly gay when this man was around, when he came to the apartment, and I knew, as most children intuit, that it was a good time to ask for things like candy money or an extra piece of pie when my mother was feeling gay, and she would be generous, then, to give me what I wanted. This tall, thin man would lean over and shake my hand to greet me when he came for a visit, slipping a nickel into it. One night, I was awakened to hear my father and this man—I think his name was Jack or Jake—yelling in the apartment. I spied through the crack of the bedroom door to watch. It frightened me, the vehemence in their voices. My mother ended the quarrel when she heard me whimpering. She picked me up from off the bedroom floor and told me that all was well, that my father and Jake were having "a friendly disagreement."

Disagreement. I'd never heard that word before. It meant loud, angry words, like my parents sometimes spoke to each other but that never amounted to anything. When I grew up I realized that my mother had used many euphemisms to describe unpleasant things.

I recall my Great Uncle Jim, on my mother's side, was with us at the table, an old man with a red face and white whiskers and muttonchops. He died not long after that night at Delmonico's, I remember, because I heard my mother say, "The last time we saw Uncle Jim was at Delmonico's." What I remember best about him was his laugh. His voice rang with laughter. Once started, it was a symphony of graduated notes leading from one crescendo to the next, with an assortment of flurries and curlicues in between. I don't think my father liked him particularly. I don't know why, but it's the impression I got. Maybe I thought he disliked him because when Uncle Jim was laughing father was not. Soon after Uncle Jim died, my father killed my mother.

So, after nearly a lifetime had passed, dressed in my good second-hand suit, I felt a strange sense of shifting time as I entered through those etched-glass doors to witness again the Victorian opulence of gleaming wood, cushy carpeting, and rich upholstery. The room of my childhood memory seemed hardly changed.

The maitre d' might even have been the same man who'd snapped his fingers in the air, signaling the host who had long ago seated my parents and me. I was instantly taken back, listening for the rustling of taffeta, but tonight there were no women present. The men were now clean-shaven, and the mood was far from gay. I yearned for a return to that long-gone innocence. Looking back at that Delmonico's night, long ago, I recognized it as a signpost marking the end of the first short chapter of my life, the end of a time when all I knew and clung to was my mother, my hand in hers as I explored the world each day.

Now, there were no jovial uncles, no beautiful women, no orchestra playing a romantic melody, just a surreal gloom that hung in the air with the wafting tobacco smoke. The main dining room was nearly empty of diners, except for small gatherings of spent-looking souls, heads bent in desperate commiseration, not in evening suits, but in their workday chalk-stripes. For some, having lost everything in just a few days—in just a few hours—there was comfort to be had in this familiar, if temporary, haven of excess and privilege that they had become accustomed to.

Delmonico's and its fashionable heyday of the last century was quickly becoming a thing of the past. All of the grand chop and oyster houses had gone with the dawn of Prohibition and the rise of the thousands of fast and easy speaks that had popped up all over town. The kind of elegance offered by Delmonico's and other fine dining establishments of the city was for the tourists, the elderly, or the fabulously wealthy citizens of the city. The youth of today had discarded Victorian reserve for the speaks and the riotous fun of the Harlem jazz clubs, where booze was the main course. These defeated sad-sacks before me, would, undoubtedly, set off from this temporary retreat for a speakeasy or would hit their well-stocked liquor cabinets when they left here. Many would say a permanent farewell to Delmonico's.

My fear could not be checked along with my hat and coat, and as I was led up the stairs to the private dining room my feet felt heavy with trepidation. But, I set my mind to the task ahead; my behavior must not betray me, I told myself, as I entered the small private dining room where my fellow club members had gathered. After one paralyzing moment when I lingered in the entryway after I caught Anthony's eye, I felt uncertain that I could maintain the outward semblance of calm to get through the night. The sight of Trevor reassured me.

"Sorry I'm late," I said, taking the chair next to Mark's at the round table. "I have just journeyed through the land of the walking dead." My choice of words was what Dr. Freud might call a *slip*.

Trevor was across from me, beside Anthony, and Mark was to his left. There was no chair were Shaw to show up, and I hoped to God he would not.

"Yes, there's been a massacre," said Anthony.

"Lots of people ruined who couldn't make their margin calls," said Daniel.

Anthony said, "My father taught me well, having suffered his own near-ruination back in the Crash of 'Ninety-three. So, I knew the signs; I saw it coming. Everybody should have seen it coming."

"I got out in September," said Mark, "after the first drop."

"Real estate is better and safer," said Daniel.

"I'm not so sure," said Mark. "But, there might be a few good buys once the dust has settled on the Street."

"That's mercenary," said Anthony, "but that's the way of business."

Trevor sat listening; I did, too, as Anthony, Mark, and Daniel discussed possible future investments. And for the next half-hour, the conversation shifted from ordering the pheasant or the capon to Mark's personal review of the new musical, *Death Takes a Holiday*.

"It's from an Italian play, about Death, who is lonely and decides to take the form of a handsome young man. He falls in love with the daughter of the elderly fellow he must take with him when he leaves. There are objections—"

"I should say!" said Anthony.

"And they sing and dance a lot?" chuckled Daniel.

It seemed to me that everything that was discussed had to do with death, from Anthony's pheasant-shooting tips learned from his father's gamekeeper on the family's Connecticut estate, to the Broadway musical—or were my nerves in such a state that everything seemed a bit macabre?

Although Delmonico's is dry, there is always a way to procure liquor, and if you reserve a private room, wine and champagne and hard liquor will be served if you make the proper arrangements or smuggle it in a briefcase. Such was the case tonight, as the waiter uncorked the Chardonnay for the capons and then the fine Bordeaux to accompany the Beef Wellington. For the hard stuff, Anthony had brought a bottle of Chivas Regal.

Listening as the conversation moved from one inconsequential thing to the next, I was struck by the incongruity of these discussions in light of the heinous crimes Trevor Hunter was convinced these men were guilty of. If there was any doubt in my mind of the validity of his charges, it was dashed away when, through the archway, I glimpsed a familiar figure. I tried to place the face with a name. Was he a public figure? Had I seen him in the newspapers? Mark provided the answer for me when he called out to him.

"Simon! Simon Strong!"

The head whipped around, and after a second, recognition dawned on the big man's face. He smiled wide and pounced forward to meet Mark, grabbing his arm and then pumping his hand with an enthusiastic handshake.

"Why, if it isn't Mark the Shark! Where have you been keeping yourself, my boy?"

Mark released his hand and pulled the fellow in close to his side, slapping him repeatedly on the back.

"Hey, big fella! You look just grand! You've been taking care of yourself?" said Mark, pulling away and then indicating Strong's substantial girth with a brisk tap to the man's vest.

"Oh, well, you know," chuckled Strong, stroking a hand down his vest coat.

"Don't mind my asking, but, how are you weathering this storm—"

"No worries," said Strong with a forced laugh. "Never believed in speculation. Goods and services is the thing! Providing real honest-to-goodness products is the way, the American way!"

"That's very patriotic!"

"Make something people want and go out and sell it."

"Yeah," laughed Mark. "Give 'em what they want."

"Right! Not this gambling business, if you know what I mean," said Strong. And then: "I'll leave the gambling up to you, Mark the Shark!" He broke out in gales of laughter that sent tremors over his tightly buttoned bulk. "I sure hope you gentlemen aren't planning on playing poker after dinner with this fella!"

"Damn you, Simon! You are ruining my plans to take these guys for all they're worth," said Mark. "Let me introduce you to the dupes—I mean, my friends."

Another round of guffaws and coughs ensued before Mark introduced us to Simon Strong, the "entrepreneur," who we all knew was the biggest supplier of booze in New York City. Goods and services, all right. He imported the good hooch and then provided the distribution services to deliver the stuff throughout the city. The Feds have never been able to make any charges stick.

"What are you doing here?" asked Mark. "This is a happy coincidence."

"It's the last Tuesday of the month. I have a standing dinner with some old Vaudevillians I used to troupe with, back in my youth. Terry Conway and Mickey O'Brian among them."

"The hobo song-and-dance men?" asked Anthony. "Oh, my goodness, when I was a kid I saw them at the Victoria! So, they're still alive?"

Strong chuckled joyfully. "I believe so. I'll have to ask them!"

I needed to know just how it was that Mark was on such intimate terms with Simon Strong, a man he'd never met, whom he had stalked one afternoon last spring and believed was the hit-and-run driver who had killed his Katie, so I just put it bluntly: "How did you and Mark meet? Was it through mutual theatrical friends?"

"We met on a *Mauritania* crossing. I don't call him Mark the Shark for nothing. This young man took me for a ride. If he hadn't saved my life—"

"That's enough, Simon," interrupted Mark.

"Well, you did. He did, you know. I collapsed sick at the game table but Mark, he saved me. I had trouble breathing and then I passed out. Mark saved me."

So Mark had lied about going to California in regard to a film adaptation of one of his books. Instead, he had sailed on the Mauritania, just as I had suspected. Had Mark tried to murder Simon Strong on the ship? Did something go wrong and was Strong granted a necessary reprieve to save Mark from discovery?

"The doc saved you, Simon. You ate too much that night, is all," said Mark. He changed the topic. "Is Helena well?"

Simon Strong's smile collapsed, and the large man appeared to shrink in his skin. Diminished corpulence.

"Helena . . . Helena is . . . better," he said, unconvincingly, and then, expanding, said, "She's crazy for you. Your visits do her good. You make her laugh. Come do that soft-shoe routine you taught her. I'm no good at it!"

"I will, Simon. Maybe this weekend?"

He nodded, almost gratefully. "It's good to meet you all; grand seeing you, Mark."

Trevor, who had been quietly observing, asked Mark, "What's the matter with his wife?"

"Guilty conscience."

Anger jolted me at the audacity of the statement. I could feel, almost hear my blood rising. His reply to Trevor confirmed to me that Mark held Simon Strong responsible for the death of Katie, that he was indeed the driver of the car that killed her. It also suggested that everybody present knew he was to blame, and that everybody was privy to Mark's plan of revenge; it had been discussed among them. Did he honestly believe that Trevor and I would keep mum if he ever went through with his plan? Through those two words he tossed off so arrogantly, Mark showed a blatant disregard for the innocent Helena Strong, whom he had befriended during the ocean crossing with malevolent intent against her husband.

As all kinds of scenarios played in my mind, Trevor touched my arm, and when I looked at him I saw a warning in his eyes. I also weighed the consequences of my outward reaction. I wanted more than anything to bolt from the room. It felt like the place was closing in on me—the potted palms, the brocade chairs and draperies. The red-embossed wallpaper took on the pattern of bloody paw-prints.

"What is it, Ernest?" asked Daniel.

"What?" I asked, reaching out from my fugue.

"You look ill."

"Do I?" I said.

"Are you in pain?" suggested Trevor, throwing me a lifeline.

"Uh, yes." I stammered. "The ribs, you know. And I'm not used to so much liquor."

"Oh, my dear boy!" said Anthony with a solicitous pout. "We need to get you home to your bed!"

"Oh, no . . . I don't want to break up the celebration. It's lovely . . . men's room. . . ."

I ran out and arrived in time to toss the contents of my stomach. I splashed water on my face and tried to pull myself together before returning to the supper party. Upon entering, I realized that they must have discussed getting me home and that Trevor had been designated my escort.

"I'll get a cab," I said. "You really should stay, not worry about me."

It had been settled, and I was glad that Trevor had arranged it all.

Once in the taxi, I settled back to regain some semblance of my usual self before returning home. I didn't want Cherish to see me like this. I worried that she would read the horror that had played in my head, and there would be questions. Questions I didn't want to answer. I was, by association, in cahoots with a murderous gang, and I had to somehow escape from the hold they had on me.

Trevor was silent until we passed Washington Square, but then he spoke.

"He's poisoning the wife. Strong's wife."

It was then that I understood what was going on.

I said, "You think he wants to punish the man by hurting—killing—his wife!"

"A sort of poetic justice, yes, I believe it might be so."

"Wait a minute!" I said, as another revelation struck me. "It was the *wife* who was driving, the wife who ran Katie down!"

"You may have something there, Ernest. But, aside from confronting Mark, how can we know?"

The taxi pulled up to the curb, and Trevor asked if I wanted company. I looked up to the darkened windows of my flat. Cherish was out somewhere; she hadn't expected me home for another few hours.

"I need to think," I said.

"Not tonight, Ernest. Get some sleep, and come to my house in the morning. We'll sort out what to do."

I walked up the stairs and entered the dark apartment. I didn't bother with the lights; I wanted nothing other than to collapse in my old armchair and to mindlessly follow the shadowy patterns cast by passing headlights along the walls until I was hypnotized into a deep sleep.

A noise, a *thump*.

Perhaps Cherish was at home, in the bedroom, reading or sleeping. I opened the door, gingerly, just a crack, to look in, not wanting to disturb her if she was asleep.

The streetlamp created a canvas of light and shadow in the dark, illuminating the bedroom in bits and pieces, like scattered pieces of a collage against a dark field: Phantom window frames elongated and were chased across the wall by passing headlights. A star pinged off the brass lamp and then skittered off into the void; a flash of white flesh, the sweep of hair, a sharp tussle, a sudden rustle of sheets, the creak of bedsprings. Cherish was in bed, asleep after all, I thought.

At her gasp of discovery, I was about to reassure her that it was me, returned early. But I had gotten it all wrong. She was not alone in our bed.

A whirring buzz echoed in my ears, and then, as if the air had been sucked out of the room, out of my lungs, a dead silence deafened me. Blinded by a head-rush, I gripped the door jamb to ground myself. From deep within my chest began the throbbing, and then the pounding, and then the unceasing drumbeat that mocked my heart. I was a knot of fried wires, shorted connections.

The realization tossed me into a great, fathomless abyss, unrecoverable.

The picture began to move: a glimpse of white breast, Cherish, covering herself. I could smell him before I saw him. Hints of linseed oil and turpentine mingled with masculine musk. Carlos!

But, no; a dark stranger, bare-chested and sweat-glistened.

I pushed past him as easily as if through a turnstile, and I reached out to engulf warm flesh. A pale eye looked fiercely into mine, as a manic force urged me on, my hands cramping from the grip I could not, would not, unlock. I couldn't let go, I couldn't. If I did, it would be over. . . .

All that I believed was good in my life, all that I had come to trust in, dissipated like a final breath.

And then a scene from long ago played before my mind's eye:

His fury contained, suddenly, after throwing her to the floor. I watched with paralyzing fear, waiting for him to pull her into his arms, to lift her to her feet, to beg her forgiveness for striking her down. But after the shock, which left her silent for a time, up rose the strident strains of her voiced outrage.

I watched from my hiding place within the cabinet, its screened panels like the divider in a confessional. My father's hand became a claw, and it flailed out and gripped my mother's neck. Her lustrous dark hair loosened and tumbled over his fingers. They moved together, a horizontal dance, like they did that night when I was scared from a bad dream and had sought my mother's comfort. I had found them, not asleep in their bed, but him on top of her, rocking her beneath him in a comforting way, I knew, because I

*heard her long, breathy sigh. I knew she had had a
bad dream, too. When his head jerked and he saw me
in the doorway, and yelled scathingly, "Get out, you
little spy!" I ran to my bed. I heard their quarreling
voices echoing through the hall.*

I watched the past as I pressed into the long
white neck.

And then, as if from some far-off place, I saw
that it was me atop the woman. It was me, not my
father, now, replaying that horrific scene, the scene
that stayed with me and had haunted my life.

Something brought me back—my mother's
wretched plea? Something, someone brought me
back to the present and to my senses.

I violently pushed Cherish away, revolted, as
if I had touched a leper. Were these sinewy things a
part of me, these bulging palms, these fingers, flexed
like talons? Why did I have my father's hands, I
wondered? Why were they now mine?

I saw Cherish. Unmoving, prone on the bed.
My panic growing as I took in the magnitude of what
I had done.

A hard blow to my back, and pain radiated
through me. I was on my face, prone on the floor,
before something fierce pulled me to my feet. I
staggered before a fist slammed into my head.

I heard the rasping cries. Hot, wet blood
blurred my vision, and despite the muffled ringing
in my ears and a new kind of throbbing in my head,
I heard the rasping cries of the woman, and rejoiced

that they came from Cherish, pleading for the stranger to end his attack.

When I regained my balance, a long time passed—although it may have only been a second—as we all looked from one to another in the gray room, appraising what might come next. They were waiting on me; it all depended on what I would do—or not do.

Suddenly, I became detached from it all. I didn't care anymore; I didn't care that the stranger was a better-looking man than I, that he wore a tattoo on his left forearm, and that his black hair curled rakishly around his ears. That he wore sex like a second skin.

I took an unconscious inventory of him, and the wanton, disheveled beauty of Cherish, and although I watched the scene play out, detached from my body, the image of them together was branded into my mind, a picture I would be powerless to look away from, one that would follow and taunt me whenever I thought of her.

It was then that I understood that I had been spiraling down to this moment all of my life. The violent legacy I had so recoiled from had reached up to snatch me and lay its claim on my soul.

We always become that which we fear the most.

Was it a look of pity she wore, or was it regret? Or was it disgust? I didn't care to know. I didn't care if she stayed or left; it seemed too late for caring one way or the other. I was ruined. Past redemption. All that mattered now was that she was not dead by my hand. All that mattered now was that *I was not my father*. And all that mattered now was that I leave the apartment.

The next thing I knew I was on the street and Anthony Young was there, following behind me. I was half running with no destination, just aimless flight, trying to escape the image of Cherish and her lover. Anthony called out as I approached Seventh Avenue. I stopped to catch my breath, the ache in my ribs punctuated with every deep inhalation. And then he arrived by my side.

"Ernest."

"What are you doing here? Why aren't you—I just left you—Oh, go away!"

"I was worried about you."

"'Were you? Why is that?" I lashed out viciously. I resented his intrusion into my private torment. But he ignored the scorn in my tone or refused to heed it.

"What's happened? What's happened to your face? Is that blood?"

"I'm not a murderer!"

"Oh?" There was a look of alarm in his eyes as his flaccid face became stone.

"I'm not—"

"What?" he said quietly as I leaned against a lamppost, overcome with despair.

I had almost said, "I am not a murderer like you, I do not have murder in me," but I had the presence of mind to know that standing before me was a danger greater than any I had encountered.

If something hadn't stopped me, Cherish would be dead right now and I would have claimed as my own my father's legacy. There was nothing I feared more than that I possessed that inheritance. This fear was a demon so great that I kept its existence hidden and securely locked away. It was inevitable that there would come a time when it would escape from the depths of my being, and that time had been tonight.

I couldn't look at Anthony Young, because I now knew all about him. I had glimpsed the evil that resided within that innocuous exterior. Where my father's grievous act upon my mother had been the tragic result of a violent passion that he had succumbed to, a terrible act that had ruined our lives, Anthony Young's deficit was that he was a callous and calculating criminal. There was no passion in Anthony, of the sort that drove my father to madness, just a seething, narcissistic desire for revenge. And for that, Anthony Young was a man beyond redemption.

If I spoke, it would just be a vacuous denial, void of any truth, full of self-pity. And as things were going for me, all I had left to have faith in was truth.

Having faced the truth about myself through this sudden enlightenment, I knew that, although I was capable of terrible things, I would never let passion rule over me again.

The old fear abated, and in its place stepped compassion. For, in an odd, unexpected twist, I felt a keen grief, once again, for the loss of my sweet mother, and along with it a twinge of what I thought was pity for my old man.

Resolved and, in a way, released, I turned to look at Anthony Young, smug in his evening clothes and his opera cloak, hand clutching his silver-handled stick, top hat angled rakishly on his head, and I watched the wily monster smile.

"Everyone's capable of murder, Ernest, my boy."

The temerity of his words confirmed his heartlessness. And, too, there was another element, something underlying the seemingly avuncular concern he was displaying for my benefit, or rather, for *his* benefit! Did he sense that I suspected what he'd been up to and that I knew of his crimes, and the crimes of the others of the club? And certainly, because I had just verbally spurned him, had he figured that I didn't approve? As if anyone in their right mind would look kindly on murder! Was he fearing that I might give him away?

I knew him better now than he thought I did, and I could see that he needed to find out if I posed a danger. He wasn't sure *what* or how much I knew. And until he was assured of my loyalty, he would play the role of the wise mentor.

I had to tread carefully. So I told him the truth: "Cherish is screwing one of her painters. I nearly killed them both."

"You caught them *in flagrante delicto*?"

"Very."

"Oh, my dear boy!"

"I need to be alone right now, if you don't mind," I said, crossing the avenue, hoping that he wouldn't follow me. And, to my relief, he didn't.

I walked toward Washington Square, mindless of any destination, mindless of the swelling cheek, the tender ribs. The park was quiet, no one around, except for a man walking his dog and a couple of NYU kids on a bench. I passed a sad specimen curled up on another, his cap pulled over his face, newspapers serving as a blanket, sleeping it off. . . .

I wandered aimlessly, and then I was passing the teeming tenements of Little Italy, crossing Canal into Chinatown, the aromas of garlic and fish and ginger and fried oil and exotic spices a testament of melding cultures. The neighborhoods were still alive with activity even this late at night.

In the past, I had often enjoyed the distractions of these streets, the little mom-and-pop eateries and bakeries crammed into storefronts and offering fare far more delicious than might be found in the elegant uptown restaurants; the markets and pushcarts with their variety of cheap goods; the colorful patchwork of nations adorning the way; the sounds of languages tripping off tongues and eluding my understanding;

the passionate interactions among the newly arrived immigrants, natural, and as yet unsullied by the strictures of American society. Here were people who had come from working their land, men and women who now were building the city with their labor and skills learned in distant places, men having gambled that here, in America, was a better life than the one they'd sailed from, only to discover that they would have to work hard for generations to come in order to mine that elusive gold from the streets.

I like to watch the kids playing stickball, see the window displays of hanging mortadellas and giant cheese balls adorning the shops of the Italians. Cross south on Canal Street and the mummified corpses of slaughtered ducklings and brilliant peppers promised feasts from Peking. On both sides of the Canal Street aisle were the men—friends, colleagues—in fervent discussion on stoops, and the women gossiping as they hung out the wash on pulley lines connecting their buildings to others, connecting their lives to others. And surrounding these streets are other blocks of streets filled with immigrants from the Ukraine and the Jews from Eastern Europe.

I suppose that because I have been alone so much of my life, orphaned by violence and sent to stay with strangers in the orphan asylum until I came of age, I find a sort of precarious comfort in observing, if not being a part of, this world and these "families" of peoples. So, for a while I had a reprieve from my troubles as my attention was drawn from one fanciful sight to the next: plastered posters of Catholic saints north of Canal, and the bobbing strings of orange and red and blue paper lanterns celebrating the Orient to its south.

When I had circled through these streets, unobserved and anonymous to their residents, except for the offer or two of the delights of the flesh as well as the mind-numbing cure of opiates, both of which I could ill afford, I retreated toward the quiet path that was Greenwich Street.

It was late and a straight haul back to the apartment above the shoemaker's shop. I walked a steady pace, now, calmer for my exertions, my aches numbed by the cold night air. My pace slackened as I turned onto my street, now quiet and still, eerily so, its residents in slumber. I dreaded my return, the not knowing what I should find, and the confrontation with Cherish.

A flicker of light, a match struck in the dark, caught my attention. A curling drift of smoke betrayed a skulking presence as it slunk into the deep shadow of a doorway. This gave me pause, and made me wonder if the glimpse of coattail was that of the man I had found with Cherish, watching, waiting for my return. . . .

I continued on toward the storefront, the window of the shoemaker's shop darkened, now, and then on toward my door. I looked up and saw the window curtain of the flat pulled shut, diffused light coming from behind it.

A candle burning for your return. . . .

I climbed the stairs with leaden feet; sadness, nothing more, filled me.

Cherish was sitting in the armchair, its back to the door. I came around and sat across from her. She looked me over, a little frown furrowing her brow, as she quickly evaluated both my injuries and my mood. For the latter, I gave her no cause for alarm. I was too spent to pose any harm to her. And she appeared unaffected by our struggle earlier in the night.

I wanted to say a million things: that I was sorry that I had so brutally attacked her, that I had been grateful that she had loved me, that I would take whatever love and affection she had to offer me, that she was the only one who made my sorry existence worth anything, that I would do whatever it took to win her back.

I didn't know where to begin my appeal, and even if I did, I couldn't form the words to tell her, to beg her not to leave me. My ineffectuality shamed me so much that I turned my eyes away from hers and waited for her to speak, for her to give me a cue where to begin. Finally, she did.

"I'm sorry that you saw that," she said, her voice a monotone.

I waited for more, but she didn't have anything to add, so I waited, silently, just looking at my hands resting in my lap, forcing back the sob that threatened to escape my throat.

"I've moved a few things upstairs to the studio. I can sleep there, so you won't have to—"

But, I was a changed man, though one still clinging to the life I thought I had just a few hours ago with the woman I loved, the woman I didn't really know. I remembered Trevor's words when I voiced my disbelief at his accusations about Anthony Young: "When are you going to realize that you can never know what is in another person's mind, in their heart?"

And I remembered his advice. "Never ask a question you don't really want to know the answer to."

But, now was a time of truth, even if I wouldn't like what I was about to hear. I knew I had to hear it, anyway. I tried swallowing the knot that had expanded in my throat, and then croaked out, "I don't understand. You said, 'I'm sorry that you saw that.'"

She looked directly at me; eyelids fluttered, an eyebrow rose up infinitesimally, as the merest trace of a smile lifted the outer corners of her mouth, and then, as if it never was, disappeared. But the "look" I knew so well, the look that bespoke a mild irritation, a look devoid of passion and mostly reserved for uncooperative store clerks and bureaucratic dullards, was enough to crush me down. I was a vulnerable child, now.

I formed my words slowly. "So, are you saying that what I saw tonight was a fluke, a onetime indiscretion, a meaningless . . . roll in the hay? That I caught you at a time that you were . . . *not at your moral best*? That you'd succumbed to something beyond your control? That it was just sex?"

The image of Cherish and her lover in passionate embrace flashed in my mind's eye and sent me to the edge. I became the belligerent child, striking out in anger, not caring what I said as long as I could release the rage within me.

"Or, did you mean you'd rather I hadn't *caught* you cheating on me tonight, and God knows how many other nights? Tell me! Did you pick him up off the street? Is he someone I should know?"

Nothing, she said nothing, just stared at me, and I read her silence as coldhearted indifference. I was nothing to her, *nothing!* And what made things worse was my own self-loathing. I was nothing because I had nothing. And now I didn't have the one thing that made life worth living. With that cruel realization, I lashed out. *"What?"* I shrieked, my pain raw, *"Does he have a bigger cock than me?"*

I knew I had gone too far when she winced. But at least it was *something*, if only a knee-jerk reaction. And although I felt a thrill of power course through me, I could not ask the most important, the most terrible and final question: *Are you in love with the son-of-a-bitch?*

"Well?"

Silence. She didn't move; her face, her eyes betrayed nothing she might be thinking. She wouldn't even give me the satisfaction of an answer, any explanation as to *why*.

Unable to elicit any response from her—of remorse, or of pity, of any attempt to regain my trust and my forgiveness—I became resigned.

After what seemed an interminable silence, I said, "All right, I have my answer."

I got up from the chair and stiffly walked into the bedroom, gently closing the door behind me. I reclaimed the bed, the bed they had dared to—. She had made it up with fresh sheets, but the quilt that she had designed was gone. Its absence said it all, all that Cherish had failed to say. Vestiges of hope still existed in my heart, so I waited to see if she would enter, follow me, come to reassure me, fight for me. After some time, I heard the apartment door closing. I fell into a dreamless sleep.

Chapter Six

I awoke to the sounds of the milkman's truck, the clinking of bottles signaling his arrival. The room was still a dark tomb.

The next thing I knew, sun was filtering in through the curtains and traffic noise was at its peak noonday volume. My head, especially my left cheekbone, throbbed against the pillow. Eyes closed, I reached out a hand in search of the suit coat I'd thrown off, which had landed somewhere atop the bedcovers. Once found, I felt for the bottle of nose-drops that Trevor had prepared for me.

Everything ached to varying degrees around my body, from sharp to dull, pain radiating from the points of impact, and it was an effort to get out of bed. *Was this what Jack Dempsey endured after a prizefight?* I wondered. Yeah, but Dempsey beat his challengers.

I was now hopelessly unemployed again, since I still could not return to the rigors of my bakery or waiter's jobs. The club waiter's job was probably gone. They hired someone else. I might be able to get it back, as the club was often shorthanded of staff. The bakery job would be history, too, if I didn't return by Thursday. Today is Wednesday. I had less than a day to pull myself together, and what was the likelihood of that? I trudged to the bathroom and couldn't avoid the pathetic face that stared back at me in the mirror. After a cursory search, I finally found the bottle of aspirin on the shelf. It was under my nose all along, but I was too wasted to see it.

I tossed back two, and cupped water with my hand after them.

Something clicked in my mind, prompted by the very act of taking the pills. Funny, how the brain works. You can be witness to something seemingly innocent, and it doesn't register as anything of significance. It takes hours, days, even, for a tiny detail to filter through the vast activity of your daily experience before it arrives at the forefront of your mind, signaling for attention.

Yes, I thought, revisiting last evening's activities at Delmonico's, I had been witness to it, but at the time, I hadn't registered the seemingly innocent little maneuver for the dastardly deed it really was! I went into the living room, to the telephone on the desk.

Last summer, Cherish had had a telephone installed. She insisted that it was important for her to be able to receive calls around the time of her gallery show. She argued that if she could get an occasional modeling job, Neysa and other illustrators needed to be able to reach her promptly. Before, we used to go downstairs to use the payphone in the shop, but now we could bear the expense, she argued, and since it was a party-line shared with another family, it wouldn't be too costly.

The problem was a Mrs. Callahan, one of the party-line users, who chattered incessantly. It was mutually decided that from the hour to the half-hour, Mrs. Callahan would have use of the line, we taking the last half-hour. Our line would ring twice in short intervals in repetition. The Callahans' ring was a single bell.

I forgot to check the time, and heard Mrs. Callahan's bleating tirade, so I hung up and checked the wall clock. It was later in the afternoon than I had thought. It read three-twenty-two. I had about ten minutes before she would hang up and I could make the call, so I returned to the bathroom to wash and shave.

I couldn't get through to Trevor. His man, Chevy, told me that Mr. Hunter was not at home, and he didn't know when to expect him back, so I left a message for Trevor to telephone me immediately upon his return.

As I waited, sitting in my armchair, looking at the various objects that made the apartment a home, I realized that the place contained a bunch of old, worthless, and discarded things, items other people had no use for, but that Cherish had collected and restored or fashioned to new uses. She was clever, and had so artfully arranged these orphaned pieces as to create a haven in a place that was nothing better than a dump to most people. And hadn't I, too, been one of her rescued orphans, reworked and made pretty and useful for a while? Just the debris of my life, this room and the man, what was left of him, sitting in the near-dark.

I got up, trying to decide what to do. Cherish wouldn't chance returning, I didn't think, unless she was sure I wasn't at home. She didn't like confrontations, and my presence would likely cause one. I felt raw, body and soul.

I grew impatient waiting for Trevor to telephone. I walked to a window, its curtain still drawn. I moved it aside to look out onto the street.

Streetlamps would be coming on soon. Lamps in the buildings across the way were lit. People hurrying along, kids trying to squeeze in a last game of marbles at the curb before failing light and mothers calling them in. Late autumn, and the days were fast becoming shorter.

I peered down from my perch above the street scene, following the anonymous lives filled with dreams and heartbreaks and joys that drove the pedestrian march of the city.

A figure across the street, standing still amid the whirl of activity, caught my attention. He leaned against a lamppost, back to me, partially blocked from my view. His fedora was pulled down low to meet the upturned collar of an old army trench-coat from the Great War. A curl of smoke was illuminated as the streetlamp suddenly came on, pooling him in light. That's when he turned around and glanced up at my window. He ducked his head, face shadowed by the hat brim. And then, flicking the cigarette to the curb, he walked off toward the avenue.

A fierce hunger gnawed at my stomach and I felt a wave of nausea. I hadn't eaten since yesterday morning and had tossed the Delmonico's dinner. Lightheadedness swept over me, which I mistook at first for exhaustion and the disorienting swelling of my face. I needed to get something to eat before I tried to find Trevor.

I wouldn't go to Marie's. There was a chance that I might run into one of the Murder Club men, and I was not prepared to deal with them tonight, knowing what I knew. I would get a hamburger at the Greek's on Seventh Avenue, I decided, checking my coat pocket for cash. Three bucks, twenty-two cents. It would last the week.

I was at the counter, finishing the last forkful of the Greek's apple pie, when a newsy hawking his papers appeared at my side. I looked up at the pug-nosed Irish kid, his cap too big for his head.

"Pay-pa, Mista?" he asked.

I took the paper and paid the nickel.

He leaned in and whispered, "Page six, ya gotta look at." And then he was chased out of the place by the Greek.

I figured there was a great story on page six. Clever way to raise a man's curiosity and sell more papers. I read the headlines first. More bad news from Wall Street and the bankers.

Missing Airliner Brought in Safely.

I asked the waitress for a refill of my coffee, and then scanned the column. Page six? What's exciting on page six? I wondered, turning the sheets of the tabloid over and creasing down the fold with the palm of my hand.

Page six . . .

Simon Horatio Strong Dead

The millionaire entrepreneur died last night at his Long Island home from a heart attack.

The words leaped off the page at me as I stumbled down the column, skipping words, entire phrases.

Heart failure . . . known heart condition . . .

All I knew was that Strong was dead and it had happened last night. Strong's murder was a *fait accompli.* I had to find Trevor. We had to go to the police.

Out onto Seventh Avenue, I headed north and was about to turn onto Barrow Street for a zigzag walk through side streets toward Sixth, when someone brushed up beside me.

"Go to Chumley's, right now."

I was about to respond, but the man—he was wearing a trench coat—walked on. I lost him when a dozen college kids poured out of an exit door and blocked him from sight. In spite of serious misgivings, I decided to follow the instruction, because it was Stephen Shaw under the trench coat.

His was a good disguise. I'd never seen him wearing anything as conventional as a fedora. His hat of choice was a fisherman's cap that needed laundering, threadbare corduroy britches, and faded polo shirts under shabby dung-colored waistcoats. I knew it was Shaw as soon as he spoke, as soon as I smelled him. It had been Shaw in the army trench coat watching my window from the street earlier today.

Dodging traffic, I crossed the avenue and went on toward Bedford Street, more than a little nervous that I might be walking into something very unpleasant. The clandestine nature of Shaw's request was unsettling, and although I loathed the despicable Stephen Shaw, Chumley's was a public house, albeit a speakeasy, with lots of people around, so I would not be too vulnerable to any real danger.

Since Trevor threw light on the men's characters, I was able to see aspects of their natures more clearly now: The charm of Anthony Young was a guise for something sinister, while Shaw's blatant audacity—his baiting of and inherent dislike for Anthony—was honest, if sometimes offensive, contempt. Shaw, although obnoxious with his bluster, was my best defense.

I walked through the narrow alley leading to the hidden No. 86 courtyard, and was met at the door by the bouncer, who told me, "Go to the *ladies.*"

It took me a second to figure out what he meant, and when I did, I headed through the bar to the ladies' room, where, when I entered, Shaw was lurking behind the door. When he bounded up behind me I was sure I'd miscalculated his trustworthiness, and he was about to attack. I raised a protective hand. But he pushed me aside and walked a few steps past the sink and toilet. There he pressed on the corner of a wall of shelving. Its frame pivoted forward and behind was revealed the hidden dumbwaiter. It was the secret passageway to the upstairs meeting room.

He told me to get in. I feared he would certainly make me if I refused. Shaw was not as tall as I, but he had an advantage of fifty pounds and the muscle of a football tackler.

Seeing my hesitation I was admonished with, "C'mon, c'mon, stop the shillyshallying and get in. We don't have all night. He's waiting for you." Shaw hustled me into the lift.

I panicked, not knowing what terrible fate awaited me. Was Shaw Anthony Young's emissary? Had the men of the club arranged this clandestine meeting? Were the others waiting upstairs? I had no plan as to how I would handle whatever situation I was thrust into. I doubted I could say anything that would convince these killers that I wasn't a threat.

And then came the jolt as the small box was drowned in darkness and I felt myself rising upward. Claustrophobia took hold. But the sensation was fleeting as light chased the darkness away and a room opened up before me.

Trevor Hunter pulled me out of the small conveyance, and sent it back down for Shaw. I suppose the look on my face was enough for him to apologize for the moments of terror I had endured.

"You're a sight," said Trevor, frowning at my face. "I'm sorry, Ernest, but this was the safest way to meet."

"I thought ... I thought it was—"

"Tony and his gang of killers?"

I nodded.

"Well, you should be concerned. You are being followed."

"Yes, Shaw's—"

"I asked him to. He's been keeping an eye on you since I spoke with him this morning. You see, last night, Anthony Young telephoned to tell me what happened between you and Cherish."

"Did Anthony tell you that he followed me home after the dinner?"

"Yes, and he said he was worried about you."

"*Pshaw!* He was worried for himself, you mean. Listen, I couldn't think last night. I just wanted to get away from him. But, I think he suspected that I wasn't just sick. I think he came after me because he suspected that I'd noticed something."

Shaw emerged from the lift and then secured it to insure our privacy from others who might try to venture up.

Trevor said, "Anthony told me you nearly killed Cherish."

"Yes, I was afraid I might've gone too far. I told him—"

I was trying to think exactly what I had said to Anthony. "Let's just say he arrived at the worst possible time. I may have babbled something because he—"

I looked back on the scene and the words we'd exchanged. I paraphrased as best I could. "I think I said that I wasn't a murderer, yes, that's what I said. And he said something like, 'We're all capable of murder.' I caught *his* meaning, which wasn't quite what *I* meant, so I made it clear I was talking about Cherish and a confrontation we had, something that was none of his business. But I'm afraid it was a weak recovery on my part. I was off my guard when he caught up to me."

"Obviously."

"So he thinks you know something?" asked Shaw. "Something that made you sick?"

"Why else would he have followed me home? To tuck me into bed? When we left last night, I knew Mark was up to something, planning something to get back at Simon Strong. It's what we both thought, right, Trevor? But, this afternoon I realized that I had noticed something, something more damning and more immediate. It was Mark's use of misdirection. I might have somehow prevented—well, maybe I didn't see it exactly, but I did see what looked like *the move*."

"Yes, I think we all watched the switch and didn't realize it in the moment," said Trevor, "but that's the rub, you see?"

"What are you talking about?" asked Shaw.

Trevor said, "Prestidigitation, Stephen. Mark's skills at sleight-of-hand are known."

"Pickpocket?"

"Magic, card tricks, and yes, Mark can pick a pocket, if he chooses," said Trevor.

"I think he lifted and then exchanged Strong's heart medicine," I said, "when he greeted the man."

"Yes," agreed Trevor, "he made several physical contacts with the old boy."

Shaw asked, "How'd he know which—"

"Strong alluded to Mark's being a frequent visitor to his Long Island estate since they met on the *Mauritania* crossing."

"So, Mark might know things like which pocket he kept his pills in?"

"Yes," I replied, "probably even what kind of receptacle they were stored in."

"I suspect cyanide was Mark's poison of choice," said Trevor.

I looked at Shaw, who was nodding. I asked, "You knew what they were up to all along?"

Shaw smirked, and if he could have, he might have spit on the floor. "There was always something about Young; there was something he didn't want anybody to know about. I figured he was a nancy-boy, for sure."

"That's why you went after him?" I said, incredulously.

"*Nah*," he scoffed, as if I were an idiot. "I don't give a shit about that. I've known many a fudge-packer from my days at sea. It was him pretending he was something he wasn't, got me riled. I found out his real name and took it from there."

Shaw leaned in close, breaking the rule of distance for conversation. He squinted and bared his crooked yellow teeth and I felt myself cringe. I stood my ground as best I could. Then he sniggered low and with vile intent. I took an involuntary step back from him as he said: "Now I'm ready to kill him, after what he did to me, but first I'm gonna have a little fun with the fucking fairy."

Trevor broke in, pulling Shaw aside. "You're not going to kill anybody, Stephen. We want to send Tony to the gallows, not you."

Shaw threw him a look of disgust, but said nothing further.

Trevor put a hand on my back as if to steady me, and then led me to the table used for covert meetings in planning the overthrow of the United States government. Ours was a covert meeting of a different kind. He motioned for me to sit.

"Tell Ernest what they did to you," said Trevor to Shaw, before adding, "They think Stephen's dead."

"That's their mistake!" he chuckled, slapping the table. "I don't die so easy!"

"Left him in a watery grave," said Trevor. "That night last week at Marie's. When Tony stormed out in a huff, and then the storm?"

"I followed Young and his little buggers followed me," said Shaw.

"Tony led Stephen to an alley and the others jumped him."

"I would've killed them all, but the bastard's walking stick knocked out my lights. Next thing I knew, I woke up at the end of a pier, a rope around my waist connected to a cement block, and then I was rolled off into the river."

"Not a nice way to treat a friend," smiled Trevor.

"They wanted it to look like something the Mob done, getting even for what I wrote about their Bronx garbage scheme."

"Wouldn't the mob have ordered a bullet in your head?" I asked.

"Those boys don't use bullets if they don't have to. Drowning is more painful. It's their signature hit."

"But, how . . .?"

"How come I ain't fish food?" said Shaw, pushing back his chair, crossing a leg, and pulling up a trouser cuff. "They didn't know about the knife I keep strapped here. Cut the rope, stayed under, and swam close to the pilings."

"You knew Anthony and the others were killing off their enemies all along?" I said, "and it nearly got you killed?"

"*Nah*, to tell the truth, I didn't know nothin'. I just knew about Young and the Harvard stuff. I liked getting a rise out of the little poser, is all."

"But, you got away."

"I hid out for a couple of days. I know where to go when there's trouble."

"But, Trevor? You went to Trevor? How did you know you could trust him?"

"I didn't know, not right away," said Shaw. "I had to make sure he wasn't a part of the schemes you boys were cookin' up. But, on thinking, I knew he was always on the right side of the law—helped the police in solving cases with his science work—and I needed to trust someone on the *inside* of the club to help me get the fuckers. I thought you were with them; I wasn't going to you."

"He showed up this morning alongside my eggs and toast," chuckled Trevor. "So we conferred and figured out that if they would kill him, they were going to come after me and you, too, Ernest. Now I see that because of your remarks to Tony last night, you are in a most vulnerable position, probably first in line."

"If you don't mind my saying," said Shaw, "it's you, Hunter, who pose the bigger threat."

"Perhaps, but I am on my guard, now. Forewarned . . . and all they say."

"They say *forearmed*," said Shaw.

"I'm that, too," said Trevor, flashing the revolver that was tucked under his coat. "Thing is, what do we do about you, Ernest?"

"That's the rub," said Shaw.

Although the question was rhetorical, I looked questioningly from one man to the other. I had no answer. I didn't know what to do. I suddenly felt stupid, weak, and totally incompetent, my mind in a dizzy spin, wondering when and how the three men would strike me down.

"Let's think this over," said Trevor, rising from his chair. He began to pace across the room, back and forth, taking his pipe from his pocket, cupping its bowl and gesturing with it as if it were lit.

"Can't we just go to the police?" I said.

Trevor stopped, and turned to me with a look of disbelief. "With what? What proof have we? We may know what they did, but how do we prove that Anthony managed to poison two men from his past living in places far apart? He's not a fool. I'm sure he's covered his tracks. After all, he's had years to plan those murders.

"As for Daniel? Murder-suicide of two of his enemies might have raised suspicions, but believe me: Mark and Young will no doubt provide Daniel's alibis for both murders.

"Mark is the only wild card, the only one who might be in danger of discovery, because you can say you saw him switch Strong's medicine. But, then, what exactly *did* you see? What did *I* see? A pat on the back, on the shoulder? For all anyone knows, Strong died of a heart attack. After all, he had a heart condition. And if I could get the Chief Medical Examiner to order toxicology, his death might be deemed a suicide. He may have told everyone that his money wasn't in the market—although we know his real business was rum-running—he may in fact have lost a bundle that he wouldn't have admitted to. He died at home, remember. Try to prove the cyanide was put there by Mark.

"Now, you are in the worst position, Ernest. Young is unsure of you. I think you have to make him believe that you are at the end of your rope. After all, you admitted nearly killing Cherish, you've lost your jobs, and Harvey Price is the cause of your tumble to rock-bottom. I think we should use this."

"What? You want me to tell Anthony I want to avenge my downfall by killing Harvey Price?"

Shaw and Tony looked at each other as if they had hit pay-dirt.

"Are you both out of your fucking minds?"

"If we can get these men into a trap—to assist in a murder plan, well then, we have them!"

"By the balls!" agreed Shaw. "It's a plan that could work, all right."

"If the murder can be set up, we can catch them at it."

'Catch *me*, you mean!"

"Don't be an idiot, Ernest. The police will be on hand to protect you, not accuse you."

Shaw leaned over the table and leveled his squinty-eyed stare at me. "What's the matter, don't you have the stomach for it?"

"Oh, stuff it!" I yelled back, and he laughed at that.

"You gotta do something. You gotta have the guts to fight to save yourself or they'll kill you, you know that! These bastards have already killed five men, and they think I'm dead, so it's six down to them. What's one more to protect their nasty secrets?"

I reached out and grabbed Shaw by the collar of his trench coat. "Shut the fuck up!" I spat out, and then pushed him away when I saw a new look in his eyes, one I'd not seen before. He relented. I was surprised that he didn't add more damage to my swollen face.

"All right. I'll do it," I said, "but what, exactly?"

"Go home, and when Tony calls you," said Trevor, "tell him you need the advice of a friend.

He'll buy that line. Then go see him at his house and tell him how miserable you are and start blaming Price for your misfortunes. If he comes right out and says that he thinks you saw something go down at Delmonico's, well, you won't be able to quell those suspicions, so admit that you did see Mark switch the bottles. Pretend to *admire* Mark for what he did, even though it turns your stomach to say so. You have the advantage of what transpired with Cherish to squash Tony's suspicions that you'd turn on the men. Take that advantage. Once a plan is hatched, we'll bring in the police. Just make sure that Mark and Daniel play an active part in the murder setup. They need to be held as accessories to the attempted murder. From there, we'll be able to effect an investigation of the other murders. Just think, Ernest, if you can do this, you will be saving a woman from execution for the poisoning death of her husband; most important for your own consideration, you'll be safe from their attempt to kill you. And so will I be, for that matter."

It was decided that I should return home for the evening and lay low and call Anthony in the morning. We went down on the dumbwaiter—Shaw first, and me behind him, after which he spirited me away through the kitchen door and out onto the street.

After a nerve-wracking walk home, avoiding the less-trafficked side streets, I nervously approached the apartment building, my eyes searching the many doorways, looking into the shadowy recesses for any indication that someone might be lurking about, ready to jump me as I walked past. I walked through the front door and climbed the stairs as quietly as possible, listening for unusual creaks that would betray an attacker. But, the music from Mr. Vitelli's radio obscured the presence of anyone who might be waiting for me at the turn of the landing.

I wondered, as I approached the apartment door, whether I would be safer locked in the flat or out on the street. In some ways, the apartment might just serve as a trap. I was about to unlock the door when I heard a noise from within. I thought that Cherish might have returned.

Then prescience washed over me, a chill skittered over my shoulders and I shivered. I removed my hand from the doorknob and slipped my key into my jacket pocket and hurried back down the stairs.

Should I walk out of the building, I would be seen from the window if someone were up there watching for me. He might have already seen me enter, I thought. Unable to brush off the feeling that I was in danger, I had to think how best to get out of the building unseen.

The cellar was my only recourse for now, its entry just under the ground-floor staircase. Through a crack of the door I might glimpse anyone who left the building.

It wasn't long before I heard footsteps on the staircase overhead. I watched Mark walking out onto the sidewalk.

Once returned to my apartment, I leaned my back against the door and did a visual scan of the living room. The curtains were closed, books on the table as I'd left them, my desk still an organized jumble of papers. Then I walked to the kitchen for a careful search to see if anything there was disturbed. Finding nothing out of place, I then checked the bathroom. The sink had water droplets near the soap holder, and because the bowl was dry I wondered if it had been in use and then wiped clean. I looked through the items on the shelf inside the medicine cabinet. I would need to go through the aspirin bottle to see if all of the pills looked right. There were bottles of iodine and mercurochrome, witch hazel, toothpowder, and liniment and other topical ointments. Any one of them might have been tampered with.

The bedroom was as I had left it. The items on the bureau were gone. The hairbrush and toiletries had all belonged to Cherish. They were there when I left the apartment for the Greek's, indicating to me that she had removed them sometime before Mark's arrival. Perhaps she had opened the door to him, and upon leaving, told him to wait for my return.

My meager wardrobe looked undisturbed and my night-table appeared as I had left it. Before leaving earlier, I had fetched from the night-table the bottle of nose-drops that Trevor had prepared for me; I patted my coat pocket and felt the small bottle just where I remembered placing it. Nothing was out of place.

Had Mark come to see me as a friend? Had he come with the news of Simon Strong's death? Had he wanted to glean, through careful inquiry, my suspicions in his involvement in the man's death? Or, had he come intending to cause me harm?

I should have confronted him, I thought.

Chapter Seven

I bolted the door, jammed a chair under the knob, and then took a hot shower before falling into bed for a dreamless sleep.

When I awoke, remarkably refreshed, I noticed that the pain in my ribs had lessened. The bruise on my cheek was a sunset-over-the-North-River pallet of yellows and purples bleeding up into my eye socket. Although the flesh was tender, it looked far worse than it felt.

The sleep had restored me in another way. My thinking was clearer. The keen, paralyzing grief I felt from Cherish's betrayal, no less acute than the death of a loved one, had subsided with the advent of the challenges I was facing. Where yesterday I was functioning on raw nerves, today I felt better able to apply my wits to conquer my problems. And I was ravenously hungry.

I shaved and dressed and was out of the apartment by nine o'clock, heading for the grocery store, where I bought bacon, a carton of eggs, a loaf of bread, and a can of coffee.

Returning home, I brewed a fresh pot of coffee and had a four-egg breakfast. I wanted to be ready to meet anything coming my way.

Once sated and on my second cup, I inspected the apartment once again. The aspirin tablets looked all right, but I tossed them, along with the tonic for upset stomach, into a garbage sack. In the kitchen, I threw out the scant dry supplies on hand—the contents of the sugar bowl, the flour—anything that might disguise a white powdery arsenic.

It was the tincture that Trevor had prepared for me that caught my attention. Since it was kept on a shelf in the kitchen and meant to be dissolved in boiling water to make a tisane for relief of my sinus headaches, it seemed to be the obvious choice in which to deposit a fair amount of cyanide. I put the bottle aside for Trevor to test. He had clearly labeled the bottle with my name, dosage, and use. Both Anthony and Trevor had taught me well about the means of delivering poisons.

My mind was on poison and murder and imminent danger, so I was on alert when I heard noise from the hall. I came out of the kitchen not knowing what to expect.

Cherish entered the apartment and looked just as surprised to see me as I was her. She looked tired and her features were drawn.

"I didn't think you were in—I'm sorry," she said, turning back to the door. I wondered, *why so contrite?*

"Cherish."

"Yes?"

"You don't have to go," I said, and I could hear the begging in my voice, and it angered me.

But, she did have to go, I realized. Not because of what had happened between us, but because she was not safe here. She couldn't be safe around me right now.

"No, I'll come back another time."

I decided it was best not to object again. But, when she put her hand on the doorknob to leave, the question just seemed to ask itself:

"Why?"

She turned to look at me, full of reproach, her hand still firm on the knob.

"Does it matter?"

I braced myself for the dreaded question. "Are you in love with this guy?"

"No."

"All right, then, yes, I'd like to know why."

She looked around the room, the way one sometimes does when searching for the right words to say.

"I just gave up. It's like there's a part of you I just can't reach. It feels like you're . . . afraid of me. It makes me feel . . . insufficient. As if you don't think me smart enough, good enough, or capable of understanding—anything. It makes for a lonely life."

"Oh, my dear. . . ."

"You go away—*somewhere*. You brood and avoid me like I'm not worth your time."

Still, fury and self-hatred combined and burst into a flaming hurt in my heart. I swallowed my humiliation in the face of the potent truth she had spoken.

"I see."

"I don't think you do, Ernest."

The Robert Burns poem came to mind and I whispered it aloud:

> *"O, wad some Power the giftie gie us*
> *To see oursels as others see us."*

"What?"

"Nothing," I said. I just stood there, my eyes focusing on the floor in front of my chair, where my shoes had worn out the fibers.

"Well, that's kind of my point."

She waited for more, and when I said nothing, she turned away to leave the apartment.

"Cherish?" I said, remembering. She looked at me expectantly. I wondered if she hoped I would stop her, meet the challenge of her accusations.

"Did Mark, Mark Wendt, a friend of mine, stop by here last night?"

The remark wasn't what she'd expected; it certainly wasn't what she wanted. But, I couldn't fix anything between us right now, in light of all that was going on around us, all that she couldn't see or possibly know about, the danger she might be in just by being here.

"I didn't see him around," she replied, and then slipped out the door.

I was left hanging. There were no immediate solutions to my big problems, and I felt hedged in. If I couldn't escape dealing with these things, then I needed to escape the apartment. I needed advice and reassurances that I would survive the night. Mostly, I needed a new plan to deal with Anthony.

Because Mark had stolen into the apartment last night, the plan to entrap Anthony had to be redesigned. They knew I was on to them.

As I couldn't risk my party-line partner listening in, I went down to the shoemaker's and telephoned Trevor from the payphone at the back of the store to tell him about Mark's visit. When I told him I had searched the rooms after Mark's departure, Trevor said that he believed that the visit had a purpose; undoubtedly, Mark had planted something lethal.

"Do not Inhale, imbibe, or apply any topical treatments. Get rid of your toothpowder, shaving cream, do you understand? Eat nothing from your cupboard."

"Wait. Would he risk harming others? Cherish?"

"Probably not . . . but, you can't be sure. It's most likely in something you use often. In the coffee grounds you brew, in a bottle of booze, you get the idea."

Shaw was stashed in one of the many bedrooms of his house, he told me, and after our talk in the secret room at Chumley's, Trevor had called in a few favors—markers, no doubt—because he had enlisted the help of several "fellows" to watch the comings and goings outside of my apartment. These "fellows," I dared to presume, were probably members of a watch gang, a network of toughs of the same nationality, who were known to patrol certain sections of the city, most often individual immigrant neighborhoods, to protect them from the threat of outside gang thugs. I wouldn't notice them around, he said, but they'd be ready to jump in, should trouble find me. Walking home, I saw no one hanging around the apartment fitting the description, but, then, I wasn't supposed to see them.

We would meet in an hour's time.

I walked to the corner to get the morning editions and then decided to make a few stops before going to Marie's. I stopped by the bakery to talk with my boss, who said he had regrettably given my route away. I stopped at the window of a used bookshop, pretending interest in the display, and then walked in, casually perusing the shelves. If anyone was following me, they would presume I was just going about my business.

I walked into Romany Marie's at two o'clock, and there was still a healthy crowd lunching. Marie came to take my order, and expressed concern about the damage to my face. I made light of it, ordered a café and one of her cinnamon rolls, and proceeded to fold back the newspaper to the employment listings, randomly circling ads with my pencil.

Two men walked in right after me, and there was something about their demeanors that made me wonder if they were on my trail, men sent by Trevor to watch over me. They both looked like stevedores wandered over from the docks. They settled at the long table at the center of the room. One accidentally caught my eye and then looked away.

Trevor walked in from the kitchen entrance, the door from the courtyard, and came over to my table. For the first few minutes we talked about the obvious: the bruise on my face, the condition of my ribs, and my search for a job. Then I asked him if he'd heard from the others. He hadn't, he told me. I knew his life was in as much jeopardy as my own. They had to figure that he had grown suspicious about the deaths of Feldman and Morrow, especially after Simon Strong's sudden demise, and that Trevor would see the connections from the dead men to those he had befriended.

If Anthony thought himself immune to Trevor's suspicions about himself, he was underestimating his friend's ability to deduce. I wondered if Anthony had something on Trevor, something sinister, a crime perhaps, from his past. Anthony was no fool. He wouldn't count on

Trevor's friendship to shield him from discovery and prosecution. But my asking Trevor about his past was out of the question, I realized, because he wouldn't tell me if there was something he wished to hide.

I asked if he was taking precautions, but he brushed off the question and said, "On thinking things over, I now doubt that Anthony wants to lure you into a plan to kill Harvey Price. It's too late for that. They know you suspect their crimes, otherwise Mark would not have snuck into your apartment last night."

Trevor also was concerned that Mark and Daniel could arrive unexpectedly at my flat. If they appeared at my door, it would probably be with mal-intent. As happened with Stephen Shaw, Anthony could not kill me and dispose of my body without help. Trevor's men, out there watching the apartment, would know what to do.

"What if they want my death to look like a suicide?"

"They might take advantage of your break with Cherish, that's true. How distraught you are, and jobless. They'd want to get you out of the apartment so there'd be no connection to them, take you to an outdoor location, like they did with Shaw. It's possible they will ask you to meet with them in a secluded location. Do something that will look like an accident. But I don't think they'd chance Cherish being at home with you, breakup or not.

"The thing is that Tony is very fond of you, and he does like the symmetry of his perfect murders. His idea of it, you know? He is just insane enough to try to lure you into the scheme to make you kill Harvey Price. He may think you vulnerable enough right now to the plan. . . . So expect him to call with his offer."

"Great. So they might try to knock me off or make me kill is what you're saying!"

"Just stay home."

"Sit in the dark and wait? Oh, for Christ's sake!"

The awesome task ahead of me filled me with overwhelming trepidation.

Trevor searched my face and asked me if I was all right. It took a few moments before I could answer him.

"No, I'm not all right! I don't know if I can do this," I said, and I could hear the rising panic in my voice. "With what's happened with Cherish, I don't know if I even care if I live or die."

"Oh, really, Ernest, you're not the first man to suffer a woman's infidelity. You must put the problem of Cherish aside and set your mind to more pressing matters."

I couldn't respond to him, I was getting choked up with emotion.

"All right," he said, and I heard his impatience growing into anger. "Well, get it over with and end your agony! Throw yourself under a truck, if you feel you must, but spare me the tired platitudes! If you're too squeamish to face the traffic, never fear, your death-wish will come true very shortly if you don't pull yourself together, man!"

Shamed, tears began to roll down my face. I was struggling not to sob out loud.

"Look, Ernest, you chose a woman whom you knew from the very beginning would hurt you in the end. She had a reputation. You know she did, don't pretend you didn't know she did. You chose her for *precisely* that reason, you know. But, before you can explore just why you feel it necessary to punish yourself, I think you have to come to terms with the fact that you didn't kill her. You are not your father. You are a morally superior, if delusional, young man."

"I'm flattered," I said, dripping sarcasm. "Am I supposed to find succor in that?"

"Not necessarily, but if it pleases your ego, why not? There's little comfort in our lives as it is."

"Thanks."

"Look, life is one big crapshoot. When are you going to learn that it doesn't always work out as you expect? That's the problem: You *expect* too much; you expect people to behave as you would have them behave. You try to infuse them with qualities they don't have, and they cannot possibly live with, or live up to, your expectations. So, when they fall out of line, you cry *foul*, and you blame them for your agony, when it's been your own fault all along, because you refused to see and hear what they've shown and told you all along. This funk you have fallen into is certainly about the boys in the club. None of them are the people you believed them to be. The boys have only compounded your misery over your disappointment with Cherish. Right now, you can't resolve things with her, but you *can* take back your life if you deal with Anthony."

All that he said was correct, of course. My nerves were fried, and I had become too overwhelmed to think rationally. I needed to take one challenge at a time. If I survived the Murder Club, I would tackle the problem of a future with or without Cherish. I reassured Trevor that my outburst had been just a momentary lapse of conviction, and that I was ready to set to the task at hand.

After Trevor had gone, I waited a while before venturing out for home, the two stevedores close behind me.

Chapter Eight

Despite my confusion and despair as I left Marie's, I became suddenly aware of how lovely the day was; it was one of those crisp autumn days, the kind that makes you believe for a time that everything is going to be fine. The sun was restorative and the brightness chased away fears of imminent danger.

I decided to lead my hefty bodyguards on a leisurely stroll before returning to the apartment. I needed to clear my head, get out of myself and my compressed little world and take in the expanse of a bigger picture, one beyond the four walls of the flat.

As I walked across Seventh and then Sixth Avenues, on my way to Washington Square, I encountered dozens of little kids, excited little clusters of them, heading home from the elementary school. Many were carrying paper decorations they had made, many wore paper headdresses, and there were flurries of brown-paper grocery bags adorned with orange-and-black images of jack o' lanterns crudely rendered in crayon. Today was Halloween, and they were anxious to get a start on their trick-or-treating campaigns through the neighborhoods. I envied their innocence and excitement. At the orphan asylum we didn't get to go door-to-door. But there was fruit punch and dunking for apples and a few ghost stories, and yes, candy, brought in by society ladies who ventured through the grim doors to distribute, piecemeal to each child, hard candy and chocolate, pencils and chalk, as we all awaited our turns.

I had never felt so alone as I did then, until now.

The rain-trees of Washington Square Park wore a yellow glow in the afternoon sunshine. I entered through the west side of the park and settled on a bench with a view of the arch.

Twenty thousand souls were buried beneath the soil of this park. . . .

I could see Anthony Young's beautiful townhouse on *The Row*, the model of grace and style of early New York, a setting depicted by Henry James in his novel about a rigid society. Through the nearly bare tree branches lining the street I looked at the low wrought-iron fences, the white Doric columns, and the small, red bricks of the house's frontage.

Would anyone guess what evil lurked behind the pristine elegance of its façade? I turned away.

I made eye contact with my escorts and headed back to the apartment.

———◆———

Eight o'clock, and still no call, no visitors. I wondered if they would wait until the middle of the night to make their move.

The telephone bell jangled two short rings and then repeated. My heart leaped, it so startled me. The sudden alarm of a telephone bell breaking the silence heralds something ominous, something disquieting, until you find out otherwise.

I picked up the receiver.

"Dear boy," said Anthony. Although he often addressed me with this affectionate greeting, tonight I imagined a menacing chill in his tone.

"Come visit me, if you will. I'd love to have a chat with you."

"Well, uh, what did you want to—"

"I've been so concerned about you, you know, with your . . . situation. I thought I might help—if I don't presume too much, that is—with a few possible suggestions that might just provide . . . solutions to these problems."

"That is very kind of you, Anthony," I said, trying to control my quavering voice. "I was going to phone you. I was in a bad temper the other night, you understand? I'm sorry. But, I don't know what can be done, except to find some kind of work, again, if Harvey Price hasn't ruined my chances, and maybe work things out with Cherish."

"Ah, yes, Cherish. That was a great shock, I'm sure."

"Yes."

"Well, she's here, you know."

"What?"

"Yes, Cherish is here, at my home. Right now."

"Why? I mean, what is she doing there?"

"Well, you know the paintings—the collages I purchased from her? They need to be expertly hung. I asked her to help me select the best places to display them. I thought perhaps in my study, but then I had to consider the drawing room, next to the Léger. There was also a space at the landing, but I was so unsure about where was best that I asked for her expertise. She's here now."

Everything was changed. The scenario that Trevor and I had imagined that the men might propose for the murder of Harvey Price had not included the possibility of Cherish. I had not imagined that she would be a pawn in Anthony's game. I was worried, now, not for my own skin, but for hers. Did Anthony think he would have an advantage over me by having her around? Was her presence intended as leverage? This was not good.

"Ernest? Are you still on the line?"

"Yes, I am."

"Why don't you come over? We can have a talk."

"All right," I stammered out. "But, really, Anthony, I'd rather see you when Cherish is not around."

"I understand. She won't be here much longer. Say, an hour?" And then the line went dead.

I dialed Trevor's number, but he was not at home, according to his man, Chevy. I asked him to tell his employer that I was at Anthony Young's and that Cherish was there.

I grabbed my coat and hat and dashed out of the apartment. I would not wait for Anthony's promise that Cherish would be gone from his home before my arrival.

The street was more crowded than usual tonight, with people of all ages in costumes and masks; parents being dragged around by their children; older kids from all over the Village scouting the apartments for treats, going to or from Halloween parties, or intent on doing mischief. A few swells from uptown in elaborate outfits and grotesque masks were in a crush to get into a café on Seventh Avenue; the band's syncopated music drifted out as I hurried to cross the intersection.

Rambunctious student pranksters owned the sidewalks along the university buildings of Washington Square. Cutting through the park, I passed a bonfire, around which danced a gang of devils and witches, undulating to the beat of tambourines and the squeals of recorders.

Farther down, closer to the arch was a figure in effigy being drawn up on a hangman's noose, thrown over an old elm. A macabre reenactment of the park's Hanging Tree where executions were performed with regularity during the eighteenth century. A hundred people were gathered around. The ghastly image of Frederick Feldman dangling from a rope in his apartment flashed through my mind. Impatient with morbid fare I circumvented the ceremony, crossed under the arch, and approached the Row.

I stopped at the gate, caught my breath, and then, remembering, turned around to see if I had been diligently tailed by my assigned team of bodyguards. I couldn't see anyone for the crowd. *My insurance policy might not be in effect*, I thought. Bracing myself, I walked up the steps to the door.

Anthony ushered me into the hall, taking my hat and coat, and then, a hand on my shoulder, led me into the drawing room.

There were Mark and Daniel, standing near the fire, like the lions flanking the public library, sipping Chivas and smoking cigarettes and looking very smug. Anthony said: "The boys just dropped in."

"Oh, you planned this, didn't you, Anthony. I am touched, really I am, that you three would want to see me through this, but where's Trevor?"

"I think he's away."

The truth was the safest way to go, so I said, "I saw him this afternoon. I was at Marie's, scouring the papers' business ads, when he came in. Where's Cherish? I changed my mind. I do want to see Cherish after all."

"She's upstairs. We've decided to hang one of her pieces in my bedroom sitting room."

"Good to see you," said Mark, putting down his empty glass, and approaching me. "Actually," he continued with a smirk as he appraised my face, "not so good. What the hell did he do to you?"

He didn't wait for my reply, but addressed Anthony. "I'm off. I've important business to attend to." He shook Anthony's hand, waved to the leonine sentinel that remained at the hearthside, and then shook my hand.

I was about to remove it when with his other hand he gripped my shoulder.

"Don't worry, friend. Everything will be all right. You'll make it all better, if you make the right choices. Listen to Tony, here. He knows what to do."

With those ambiguous remarks he left the room.

"Drink?" offered Anthony.

"No, thanks. Will Cherish be long? Does she know I'm here?"

"I didn't tell her. Now, Ernest, don't be cross with me. Come, sit down, and let me tell you my plan."

He offered me a chair and then sat across from me. I thought he was about to start his proposition when he suddenly looked over at Daniel. I saw a silent communication pass between them.

"Excuse me, gentlemen, I've a telephone call to make."

"Use the phone in the library, would you, Danny?"

When he was gone from the room, Anthony looked at his hands, which were folded in his lap. A very serious frown crossed his brow, and his flaccid chins collapsed like a wind-spent accordion to rest grimly on his chest.

And then, eyes darting up to fix on mine, he said, "You have two choices."

"I wish I knew what they were," I said with the suggestion of a laugh in my tone.

"There's no point pretending you don't know what's been going on. We know you do. What saddens me is that my protégé is not on board."

That he called me his *protégé* sickened me. But, I hadn't expected him to drop all pretense for a direct appeal, and because he had me in his home, his web, he had the advantage. And Cherish was somewhere in the house, making it all the worse.

"I want to see Cherish, Anthony, right now."

"I told you—"

"I know what you told me," I said, getting to my feet, "but I want her down here with me right now." I began to cross the room, saying, "I'll find her myself," but Anthony stopped me.

"I wouldn't do that, if I were you."

I turned at the threat and there it was, a pistol in his hand, pointed at me and held as casually as he might a snifter of brandy.

"Are you going to shoot me?" I asked, smiling and trying to assess what my next move should be. Did I risk a bullet in my back? I doubted he would risk a bloody mess on the magnificent Aubusson rug that graced the parquet. I decided not to chance it.

"Sit down, for God's sake! This is for your own good, you know."

"Oh, sure," I said, "shooting me in the back is for my own good."

"Don't get smart with me, boy."

"I can't, it seems. You have the gun."

"As I was saying, you have two choices: Kill or be killed."

"I'm a threat, is that it? I know too much. I know what you maniacs have been up to while I've been away, so you plan on killing me, too, right?"

"I certainly hope not!" said Anthony, eyebrows raised and a little smile of amusement on his lips. "It is because of you that we are all together, my boy!"

"So it's my fault."

Before he could answer, Daniel returned with Cherish at his side.

"Ernest," she said, a look of dismay mixed with surprise flashing across her face. "Did you follow me here?"

Anthony, hiding the weapon between his leg and the arm of his chair said, "I invited him. I thought we could all have a little talk."

I whispered, "Keep her out of this, Young. She knows nothing!"

"But, she is a part of this."

"What's going on? What's this all about?" demanded Cherish, not grasping the sinister aspects of the gathering. "Mr. Young, if Ernest and I wish to discuss our problems, we will do it in private, if you don't mind."

"There's nothing to discuss, anymore, is there Ernest, my boy?" said Anthony, looking over at me. "You options are: murder-suicide or the elimination of Harvey Price."

Cherish's confusion began to turn to panic. Backing away toward the arched entrance, she was met by the strong grip of Daniel Cousins.

"I'll admit I miscalculated you, using your history as a measure of character. Oh, yes, I make it my business to know everything about those I associate with. I even understood your reluctance. It made you weak. But now is the time for empowerment!"

"What is he talking about?" said Cherish.

"But we've not much choice, Ernest."

"Ernest! What is he talking about?"

"Only that murder runs in his family," said Anthony.

"Shut the hell up!" I yelled.

Anthony ignored my protest. After all, he had the gun.

"Now, I don't believe you wish to shoot the woman who betrayed you any more than you wish to kill your nemesis, your esteemed publisher of smut, Harvey Price. If not him, you see, Cherish must die by your hand, and then, in terrible remorse over what you have done, you kill yourself."

"These men are mad!" screamed Cherish, wild-eyed and appealing to me.

"Yes, darling, they are mad."

"That you two should have had this timely breakup is pure serendipity, wouldn't you say?" he said with a chuckle.

"Sit her down, Danny. Her hero is champing at the bit, if you'll excuse the cliché, even if it's apropos? And he needs to pay close attention."

"Don't you dare touch her!" I yelled, ready to leap to shield her body with my own.

"Don't be so dramatic. Of course, your show of chivalric sacrifice may be a way back into her heart. See how he loves you, my dear?"

I tried to think how I could get the gun away from Anthony. He had remained seated in the wingchair, the weapon hidden from Cherish. I was standing in a direct line between them, and

Daniel stood beside her. I had to make a move, but I couldn't leave Cherish exposed.

"All right, I'll do it."

Daniel said, "You'll kill Harvey Price?"

"Yes, I understand."

"You can't turn us in without incriminating yourself, you see?" said Daniel.

"That's the idea, right?"

"You agree, then? Price is to die?" said Anthony.

"Yes. The man deserves it anyway after what he's done to me!"

"Good. It's a good alternative to shedding your blood, and that of your lovely lady. And as you say, it will keep us bound together, won't it?"

In that instant I knew that neither Cherish nor I would make it out alive, because Cherish now knew the men's secret. I wished I had never insisted she be brought into the room. And then I realized that they wanted her present and the reason why.

"Tell me what to do. How will I go about it? I'll do what you say."

I was about to add, *But Cherish leaves right now,* but stopped myself.

"Ernest, Let's be frank. I know you don't possess the intestinal fortitude to actually kill someone by your own hand, that's by your own admittance, so that is why we've called you here tonight."

"I don't understand," I said, moving closer to Anthony.

"We will do it for you," he said.

Daniel took a couple of steps to stand closer behind me, a smile on his face, looking at Anthony for approval or consent, and then Anthony nodded at him to speak:

"It's in play right this minute, uptown at the Melville Club. It was my idea. A clever one, at that, once you hear it," said Daniel. There was a diabolical trill in his voice.

I waited to hear more of what Daniel had cooked up, but once again he deferred to Anthony. At his nod he continued:

"This morning, Price received an invitation to the club—the Melville, the one where you work as a waiter a couple of nights a week. It was for him and a guest to dine there. The invitation was from a club member—who's out of town, by the way, although Price doesn't know it. It's all been arranged, you see. Price is there right now."

"And I'm to go up there—?"

"No. You would screw it up. No, you don't need to do a thing," said Daniel. "Mark is up there right now, working as a drinks server in the lounge—"

"But, how's he—"

"Tonight is Halloween, and they were understaffed. A private party or something going on at the club. Mark arranged it all. He called pretending to be you asking if you could work tonight. *And!* because all the waiters are in harlequin costume and masks, it being Halloween, no one will suspect it is Mark and not you serving drinks. A little cyanide slipped into Price's glass, and it's all done."

"But they'll think I did it!"

"Not at all. You've been with us all evening."

"But, I'll be the first one they look at. Everyone in publishing, all the newspapermen know what Price did to me, how I lost my job at the paper, and that gives me motive for killing him!"

"We are your alibi!" said Daniel, with as much excitement as if he won a jackpot.

"Yes," said Anthony. "Think about it this way, my boy. Price has a number of enemies, not just you! And there are a hundred or so people at the club tonight, any one of whom might have poisoned him. A lovely plan, don't you see?"

I thought, *they want the murder to be pinned on me.*

Their plan was to kill us, not just make me responsible for killing Price. They were going to stage a murder-suicide after Price's death. It would not happen in the house, drawing attention to my association with Anthony, but somewhere else. The scenario: I had been in despair at Cherish's betrayal, gone mad and killed the man who had ruined my career, and set on a killing spree, murdering Cherish, before shooting myself in the head. From this point forward, I was buying time.

He awaited my reaction. Daniel, in a gesture of perverted friendship, laid a hand my shoulder. I turned my head away to look at Cherish seated behind me, an expression of horror on her face. Our eyes locked, hers imploring, mine rapidly shifting to the floor, then back up to meet hers. I repeated the tiny movement and prayed that she understood my signal.

It's hard to describe, but from somewhere outside of me—or was it from within me?—a feeling of calm engulfed me and I was empowered with a primal energy. In this moment of clarity, I was released from the crippling demons of my past. I knew no fear or doubt, and what happened next all happened in an instant when the telephone rang. It broke through the silence of expectancy, and the close proximity of the urgent and piercing bell startled all of us.

I reached over and grabbed the hand that Daniel was resting on my shoulder and twisted it violently. Anthony hesitated, shakily raising the gun at me as I swung Daniel around as a shield.

Anthony fired. Daniel cried out as blood spurted from his arm.

The telephone bell rang on and on, a maddening and insistent alarm.

Anthony rose from his chair, taking aim at my head. I pushed Daniel toward him as he fired off another shot.

The two men fell back, Anthony's head hitting a marble column of the fireplace, the gun flying from his hand.

I retrieved the weapon, and turned quickly to find Cherish, whimpering and trembling uncontrollably on the floor behind her chair. "It's all right, it's all right," I managed to assure her before returning to the two men sprawled out before me.

Daniel didn't move; I presumed he'd suffered a fatal wound. Anthony may have just been stunned, knocked out, I couldn't be sure. But it wasn't my blood pouring into a pool on the Aubusson.

I lifted a wimpering and incoherent Cherish from off the floor, brought her to another part of the room, out of sight of the bodies, and sat her down on a chair. When she finally released my arm, I poured Scotch and made her drink it down, while keeping an eye on Anthony, should he revive with more tricks up his sleeve.

There was no time to waste. Racing up to the Melville would be pointless. I might never make it in time, so I headed for the telephone.

Before I could get to it, there was a fierce and relentless banging at the front door. I didn't want to waste the minute it would take to go to the door, but when I looked toward Cherish, I saw that she was on her feet and headed for the front hall. Trevor and Shaw crashed into the room, their eyes wild, Trevor brandishing his revolver, Shaw his, my bodyguards bringing up the rear.

There was no time to explain as they assessed the scene before them. I dialed the number of the club from memory, waiting ring after ring for someone to answer. When finally they did, I tried to steady my quavering voice to say that it was urgent that I speak with Harvey Price, a guest at the club. "There's been a terrible accident. It's urgent he come to the telephone immediately."

As I waited for Price to be paged, I briefed the men of the events leading up to their arrival, particularly about the plot to poison Price. Trevor was evaluating Daniel's injuries, and Anthony Young appeared to be reviving as a husky voice blared out from the telephone receiver. "Price, here! What's the problem?"

I wanted to laugh from joy and relief. Price was still alive, the bastard!

For want of any planning, and rejecting the idea that telling the truth would get him out of the club, I said, "This is Detective Donovan from the Eighteenth. There will be a car outside the front entrance of the club momentarily to escort you to New York Hospital, where your wife has been brought after suffering an accident. Best you leave immediately."

I replaced the receiver and considered my next move.

Trevor was standing over a bloodied Anthony, returned to his usual chair, and Shaw was holding his revolver on him. Daniel was dead.

"We've got to stop Mark. He may still have time to kill Price. Mark doesn't know anything that's happened here."

I quickly told Trevor what was going on and my attempt to get Price out of the club.

"Where is this club?" asked Trevor, and I told him.

Trevor grabbed the telephone receiver and told the operator it was an emergency and to connect him to the 18th precinct and a particular chief of his acquaintance.

I went to Cherish, who smiled wanly and said she was fine and then whispered to me, "Go, do what you can to stop Mark."

Police officers, responding to a neighbor's call of gunshots from Anthony's row-house, entered, and we were told to remain in the room. Trevor was back on the telephone calling the home of the Police Commissioner to set things in motion.

I couldn't wait for others to take action. As another batch of police officers entered and they were busy talking with Trevor and Shaw and Anthony, I eased out of the room and down into the street, unnoticed, and headed for Fifth Avenue and a taxi to bring me uptown to the club.

Chapter Nine

There was surprisingly little traffic as we sailed up Fifth and then turned west onto Forty-Fifth Street. I tossed my last buck at the cabbie and quit the taxi half a block from the Melville Club entrance.

A police car was parked outside the club, and standing alongside it was Harvey Price.

He was alive.

My relief was short-lived when I caught sight of a figure striding out from the service entrance of the Melville Club with the sure grace of a dancer. In a familiar topcoat and hat, and still wearing the harlequin mask, Mark Wendt turned onto the sidewalk heading east toward Fifth Avenue.

There was no time to alert the police officers. Mark had not seen me, so I had the advantage. I ran the short distance toward him, leaped at his back, threw him to the ground and pinned him with the weight of my whole body.

Around that time, Trevor and Shaw pulled up in a cab.

Police officers brought Mark to his feet. A police car, its siren whining, pulled up to the curb, followed by a cab screeching to a stop, newspaper reporters and photographers tumbling out its doors.

I was being held by one of the officers, who demanded an explanation for my attack on Mark. Mark, having no idea what had transpired in Anthony's drawing-room, began accusing me of poisoning a drink order for the publisher, Harvey Price. He said he saw me put something in the man's drink, and was trying to stop me from leaving the club.

As I protested handcuffs, the blinding light of camera flashes chronicling my moment of shame, Trevor and Shaw rushed up to meet me and there was a new round of flashes.

Recognized by a detective, Trevor quickly explained that it was Mark who had made the attempt on the life of Harvey Price. After a few moments of heated dispute, another squad car arrived and yet another detective joined the huddle, confirming the Police Commissioner's dispatch to follow Trevor Hunter's lead.

I was immediately released.

Just then a thought struck me, followed by another and still another:

Mark had indeed laced Price's drink with poison; he would not have left the club before he accomplished the delivery of the drink. And he wouldn't want to stay at the club any longer than necessary *after* delivering it to Price, for fear of discovery. Since Harvey Price was being safely tucked into the back of a squad car when Mark made his escape through the service alley, as far as Mark knew, Price had belted down his drink and was lying dead in the lounge.

This led me to the mind-shattering conclusion that there remained a deadly beverage about to be quaffed by some unsuspecting gentleman.

"This way!" I yelled out, and I saw in Shaw's expression that he had arrived at the same conclusion. My alarm had also been heard by the newspapermen.

I ran through the entrance, pushing past the doorman, the host, and a policeman chatting with a club member. Shaw was on my heels, reporters were jockeying for position, and then the cops joined in, bringing up the rear.

I knew my way around the club, and as there was no time to waste, I calculated where Price had most likely settled: the Clipper Lounge, where Price and his guest would have retreated after dinner for coffee, cigars, and prohibited and procured beverages.

I took the stairs to the second level, a thunder of boots behind me, and sprinted along the balconied hall and then into the lounge, my entourage on my heels.

Dozens of inquisitive expressions looked up in search for the cause of the ruckus. I scanned the faces staring at me, hoping to identify the man whom Price had brought as his dinner guest.

Of course! I thought when I saw him in the far corner, holding a Scotch glass in his hand.

It was John Mitchell, Harvey Price's publishing partner, and he was bringing the glass up to his lips. Our eyes locked, and I pointed at him before raising an agonized plea from across the room.

"Stop!" I cried out. "Mitchell! Put down that glass!"

I stumbled around the tight arrangement of chairs and tables to get to him before the glass met his lips. There was an abject look of horror on his face upon seeing me coming at him in what must have appeared a rabid attack and he released the glass before taking a defensive stance behind his leather club-chair.

I watched as the glass tumbled out of his hand to bounce soundlessly on the thick green carpeting, splashing its contents.

And then his hand went into his coat and another object appeared, a pistol, which he aimed at me.

"Don't come any closer!"

Police officers closed in to shield me and take away Mitchell's weapon; cameras flashed and reporters were penciling notes, taking down quotes, and trying to build a story for their morning editions.

Shaw shouted out that everyone must put down whatever they were drinking.

A few made light of the order, asking if a private club was being raided and if the Feds were on their way. A couple of others belted down the remains of their booze in defiance. A few men laughed, asking what the joke was all about, some complained begrudgingly, others demanded explanation, but most complied when another gang of police officers entered the lounge and they saw the seriousness of the order.

"Price left," said Mitchell, eyes wide with the idea that I was there seeking retribution from his colleague. "Called to the phone and sent back word he had to go off. His wife or something. I don't know where he is!"

"That drink," said Trevor.

"What about it?"

"Where's the glass Price ordered?"

"The one on the floor, goddamn it! The one I was about—what's going on here?"

"Are you sure that was the glass delivered to your friend?"

"Yes, damn you! Harvey left a perfectly good single malt untouched, and it would have been a sin to waste it," he replied to Trevor, who had retrieved the tumbler, which still contained a couple of drops of liquid.

"Son-of-a-bitch!" I said, dropping into the chair next to Mitchell. I was not aiming my remark at anyone; the swear was simply one of exasperation.

The adrenaline rush of the past few hours had finally exhausted my strength.

John Mitchell, still without a clue about what was going on, turned to me and said, "You frightened me! I know what Harvey did to you, and it wasn't nice, but you can't go around—" His rebuttal was interrupted by Stephen Shaw.

"You and your partner should be on your knees kissing this young man's arse." Shaw leaned in closer to John Mitchell's face, grabbed his finely tailored lapel, and hissed, "He just saved both of yours, you slimy toad."

Epilogue

One can become famous overnight in New York City. All you need to do is get your picture in a newspaper. The more papers on which your face is plastered, the greater the fame. Often, it means notoriety; in my case, it meant I was the hero of the day.

Front-page coverage makes you a star, and when all twelve dailies feature your mug on page one, the world comes a-calling.

There is the flash-in-the-pan famous—it usually means that the photographer caught you doing something stupid and so you wind up in the human-interest columns. But, when you break five murder cases, expose three attempted murder plots, rescue a beautiful woman from a mortal fate, vindicate a battered housewife in Detroit of poisoning her husband, *and* your face is on that venerable front page, you can pretty much write your own ticket—for about a week or so.

I became the hero of the week, the darling of the columnists. Everybody wanted to know how I foiled a pack of murderers—singlehandedly. The fact that I couldn't have done anything without the help and support of Trevor Hunter and Stephen Shaw didn't seem to matter to the press boys, no matter how much I attested their part in it. It appears that I was the most photogenic of the trio, and was seen as a dashing figure, so I bore the coverage with a certain degree of embarrassment while Hunter and Shaw were depicted as mere sidekicks.

Soon the papers would shift their focus on the remaining duo of diabolical killers, once their murder trials began. There would be revealed the ways and means by which the murders had been committed. Perfect murders.

I think of the premise posed by Dostoyevsky that Anthony had referred to: *A criminal is caught because at the time of his crime he loses the ability to reason.*

Anthony didn't take that advice to heart. As I see it, those men had lost the ability to reason from the onset. Call it *hubris*. It was hubris betrayed them.

Perfect murders, my ass.

Even as our spotlight in the press is fading, my "sidekicks" and I are sure to pop up again in the news as key witnesses at the murder trials. Anthony's and Mark's trials, that is. Daniel is quite dead. We are all known as members—the good ones and the bad—of the notorious Murder Club. The newspaper editors liked the sensational ring of the words splashed across the front page: *The Notorious Murder Club!*

And so, because of my newfound fame, I've been offered many proposals both financial and romantic. My fan mail rivals John Gilbert's. I have become a hot commodity, according to publishers who want my story and offer book deals with ridiculously inflated advances. My face was on the cover of *Time,* and I've been offered my own byline as a crime columnist for the *Daily News,* the same rag that fired me a few months ago. And I am told that the tawdry sex books I wrote for Price—the first editions—have become collectors' items and are fetching exorbitant amounts. Oh, and Irving Thalberg asked me to do a screen test. Supposedly, I have "something," whatever that means.

What do they really know?

As far as a future with Cherish? I don't know yet. I've spent much time considering how we could move forward. I've agonized. I've replayed in my mind what she had said to me that day in the apartment when I asked her "why," and she replied, *"I just gave up. It feels like you're afraid of me . . . and it makes for a lonely life."*

I know now what she had meant. I had been circling her life tentatively, carefully editing out anything that might show my vulnerability because I feared trusting her with the truth about my past. I couldn't take the risk. And it rendered me lonely, too.

But is that really all of the truth? Who am I fooling? There is an honest, although shameful, reason for why I kept a distance, besides my tainted history. I've been a coward, afraid for her see my inadequacies for fear of rejection. Perhaps what she really needed most, was brave, unguarded intimacy. She needed me to love her without fear of loss. . . .

The day after the night at the Melville Club, Trevor and his man, Chevy, helped move my scant belongings from the apartment over the shoemaker's to Trevor's Ninth Street townhouse, in which I was installed in the third-floor suite. Here, I would be able to gather my thoughts and my life and resume my career as a writer. Here, I could reflect on the course I would take with or without the woman I still loved.

As I fastened the lid of my steamer trunk and Chevy carried out my Royal typewriter, I asked Trevor, "Is there no hope for us?" I was referring to Cherish and me.

But he must have thought I was engaged in some pointless existential musings, for he replied:

"Hope is just stagnant wishful thinking. But courage! Courage makes it possible for a man to soldier on, to explore new paths. Just remember, we all die in the end, so there is not much else in life to be afraid of. Now let's get out of here," he said, shepherding me out of the apartment and into the back of his car.

The End

About the Author

Agata Stanford is the author of the humorous Dorothy Parker Mystery series. She lives with her family in New York..

.

www.ingramcontent.com/pod-product-compliance
Lightning Source LLC
Chambersburg PA
CBHW020358030726
47496CB00007B/2204